A DIVIDED RIVER
TALES FROM VASINI I

Christian Ellingsen

Copyright © 2017 Christian Ellingsen

All rights reserved.

ISBN: 1546499016
ISBN-13: 978-1546499015

Printed by CreateSpace

For Marc & Vicki

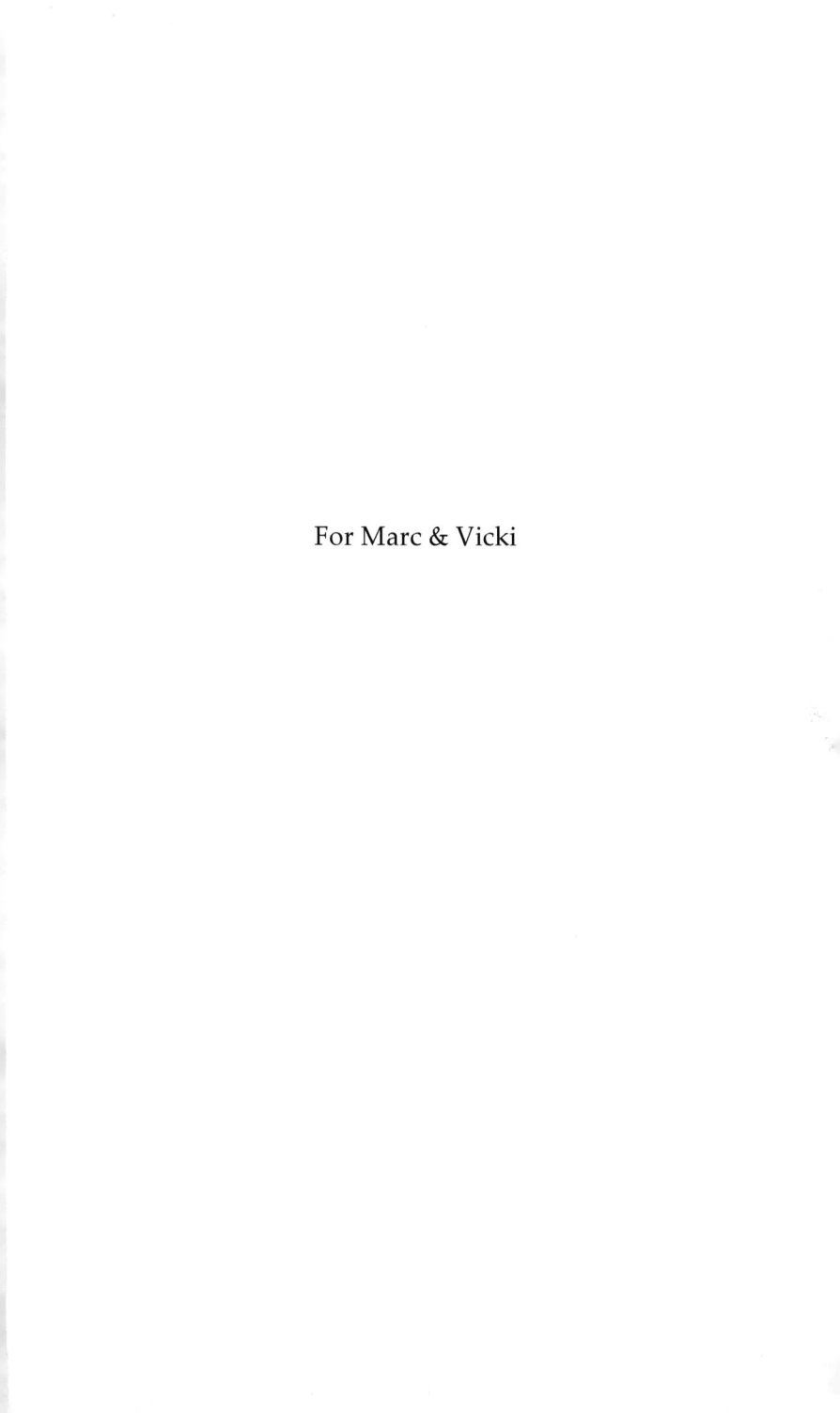

A QUICK NOTE ON CHRONOLOGY AND OTHER THINGS

Welcome to the city-state of Vasini.

For some of you, this may well be your first time — welcome. Don't panic, it's not that dangerous, just be careful what colours you wear.

For those of you returning to Vasini's streets, you may very well be asking two connected questions:

- Are Doctors Marcus Fox and Elizabeth Reid and the other characters from the *The Vasini Chronicles* novels in these stories?
- Where do these stories fit within the chronology of Vasini?

The *Tales From Vasini* short stories and novellas — this is hopefully the first of several books that will pop up between releases of *The Vasini Chronicles* novels — won't feature Fox or Reid and are unlikely to feature many of the other key characters from *The Vasini Chronicles*. They *may* appear in passing or be mentioned (after all they exist in the same world), but these stories aren't their stories. The *Tales From Vasini* — in this instance *The Mudlark's Tale* and *The Winter Fayre* — are a chance to explore the wider world and adventure through those city streets and places outside of the city where Marcus and Elizabeth don't go.

So where do these two stories sit in relation to *The Silver Mask*?

- *The Mudlark's Tale* starts in Aprilis, 195AL, approximately six months before *The Silver Mask*, which was set in December, 195AL.
- *The Winter Fayre* is set on 22nd Mortemis, 195AL, about two months after *The Silver Mask*.

The names of those months won't make much sense to you, but let me introduce to you a page from *Brightman's Almanack* — Vasini's leading miscellany of information — which will hopefully make things clearer.

Christian.

A Divided River

Brightman's Almanack 195AL

The calendar since the Fall of the Deities

Days of the week
Trad. names   Cmn. names
Primidi....................Monenday
Duodi......................Duaday
Tridi........................Treday
Quartidi..................Quarday
Quintidi...................Kinday
Sextidi.....................Sunanday
Septidi.....................Samday

Festivals of the year
Year's Birth
1st day of Novulis
Celebration of the Fall
1st day of February
Spring Festival
By the comte's decree upon the return of trade to the city. Most often on 8th day of February.
Alder's Day
18th day of Sextilis
Founding Day
8th day of September
Festival of Games
22nd day to 29th day of September
Harvest Festivals
By the decree of individual farm owners between 23rd day of December and 29th day of Mensesis.
The Winter Fayre
By the comte's decree upon the freezing of the Sini River and Hibourne ditches. In 194AL ran from 23rd day to 30th day of Mortemis.
Year's End
30th day of Mortemis.

Months of the Year
Winter
Novulis.............29 days
Seculis..............30 days

Spring
February...........29 days
Aprilis..............30 days
Quintilis...........29 days

Summer
Sextilis.............30 days
September........29 days
October............30 days

Autumn
November........29 days
December.........30 days
Mensesis..........29 days

Winter
Mortemis..........30 days

One year is 354 days.

Other events
Débutante season
Quintilis

Elections (when required)
September

(Cont.)

THE MUDLARK'S TALE

The Sini River, Southport district

Ned gripped the knife tight as he searched, pulling down his cap to guard against the chill. He wouldn't be caught unawares. Not like four nights ago. His arm still ached where he'd been cut, his chest tender and bruised black from the fist blows. He'd been stupid and lost a night's pay because of it. Laid up as he'd been with his wounds, he'd missed three nights on the riverbed and, when able to ease his aching body out of his shack, he had sold his hair to make sure he'd have food.

The low-tide lapped at his boot heels as he cast the lantern light over the mud, looking for the tells of items washed down into the river by Vasini's incessant rain — a glint, a protuberance.

Nothing.

He pulled his feet from the sucking mud and moved on, trying to keep his distance from the glows of the other mudlarks' lanterns. *Stupid. Too stupid letting 'em get the drop on me.* It had been good pay too, a couple of rings and a tobacco case.

A twinkle amongst the black quagmire of the exposed riverbed.

He moved forward slowly, hoping not to alert the other 'larks to his find, keeping his eyes on the other lights.

Whatever it was continued to twinkle, beckoning him.

The chill wind off the sea bit through his clothes, his flesh bunching at its touch. He tugged his hat lower, pulling the lapels of his coat tighter round his neck and face.

A few feet more; a few moments more.

The other 'larks continued to keep their distance.

He reached the spot and lowered his lamp, glancing down at his feet where the twinkle lay.

It was glass. A broken bottle.

Ned nudged at it with his foot in disgust, kicking it out from the mud and causing it plop down in a shallow puddle.

A shiver went through Ned.

Part of his mind tried to force his body on.

It remained there shivering, wanting to just drop to the mud but kept rigid by the cold.

Gotta move. Gotta eat.

His foot edged on through the mud.

His arm pulled the lantern up, casting the light further across the riverbed.

His eyes flitted across the black and grey scene, searching for the elusive twinkles.

He stepped forward again. As he went to drag his other foot forward, it caught. He stumbled, recovering, instinct twisting him to try to find sight of the rock that had caught him out.

The light fell on the ground behind him.

A twinkle of light.

Other 'alf o' the bottle.

Ned went to turn away. But something else glinted. Snaking out from the first twinkle.

He lowered the lantern, trying to see the object.

It was thin and less than a foot long.

He crouched down, pocketing his knife to free a hand. He reached forward, cautious of anything sharp or hidden beneath the mud.

He pulled up the object, pulling the glinting glass with it.

A chain. Could have been copper. Maybe gold or silver. Difficult to tell in the light and with mud oozing down it. And from it dangled a glass pendant, half caked in mud.

Ned had seen enough. It was something with at least some value. He thrust it into a pocket deep inside his coat and hurried to pull out his knife again.

He tried to steady his breathing as he thought, casting looks towards the other lights, checking he hadn't been spotted. If he stayed he'd risk being caught again. But if he went now another 'lark might trigger to his discovery. Realise why he was going and follow.

Ned stood, head bowed, trying to work his way through the conundrum. *Stay or Go?*

His feet edged on towards where the river still flowed.

Stay for now. Stay for now to make it look like he'd found nothing. Then leave soon; make it look like he'd given in for the night.

He pulled down his cap once more, pulling up the scarf round his face. He may have had to eat, but having his hair would have made the chill that much more tolerable.

Baker Row, Everett's Green district

No 'lark with any sense kept their pay at their shack. It was known that anyone foolish enough risked being beaten and cut in the night and having their pay taken while they lay in their own blood. Every 'lark who survived more than a week had a hidey-hole to stash their pay — a 'lark's bank as some liked to call them — preferably two or three, so it was more difficult for the less honourable to find the pay. It often meant travelling outside of Southport, to one of the other districts of Vasini, and meant that a long night was made longer. But it was the safest choice.

Ned's preferred hidey-hole was a narrow alleyway off Baker Row. It meant crossing from Southport to Everett's Green, but it was closer to his preferred broker's shop for when he would try to sell his pay the next day.

Ned flashed glances at either end of the alley, before he drew out the chain and pendant. He pulled a cloth from a pocket and wiped the mud from his pay, lowering it into the light of the lantern at his feet.

The sight brought a smile to Ned's face. Gold. Almost certainly gold. He'd get good money for it.

He looked at the pendant. The top was clear glass. Just glass. Certainly not crystal. But the bottom, it was dark. Black even.

He lifted the pendant closer, holding it sideways. The blackness flowed along the glass.

Liquid.

The damn thing had liquid, a black liquid, in it.

Ned looked at where the chain met the pendant, searching for some way to get to the contents.

The chain fed into a cap on top of the pendant, a delicate clasp to keep it shut.

Ned dug a brittle, chewed nail into the clasp and flipped it. He licked a patch clean on his thumb and placed it over the opened pendant, tipping the pendant to leave a dab of its contents on his thumb.

He sniffed, and then licked it.

His mouth twisted at the taste.

Ink.

He spat, trying to clear the taste from his mouth.

Not worth much. Not in so little an amount. But the chain. The grin returned to his face.

He closed the clasp on the pendant.

Looking at the alley entrances again, he reached up amongst the overhang of the building, his aching ribs protesting at the movement. He rummaged along the long beam, fingers searching for the touch of leather, pulling on the small satchel hidden there.

He pulled it down, flipped the flap of the satchel and slipped the chain in.

The satchel was on the beam, he'd gathered his lantern and was walking out of the alley within two breaths.

Ned's shack
Mudlarks' Way, Southport district

The tide had returned by the time Ned reached his shack. Beyond the shantytown of Mudlarks' Way he could see masts moving, sailors' calls drifting across the waters.

His shack was small, but all he needed. A pot above the fire, a stack of wood, a small bed with straw mattress and blankets. He doused and hung his lantern and stripped down to all but his cap, placing his clothes in a chest. Once his knife was placed under the bundled sheet he used as a pillow, he got into the bed and stretched out his aching body, pulling the blankets tight around him.

Ned was soon asleep, dreaming of looking for the golden chain someone had taken from his hidey-hole.

Whitmore's pawnshop
Plowham Road, Everett's Green district

Whitmore's was four streets from Ned's bank. The broker's shop sat between a tavern and a cobblers on Plowham Road. Noah Whitmore was hidden deep within the shop, amongst the rows and piles of pots, pans, clothes and other paraphernalia.

Whitmore didn't look up from the thick book propped before him on the desk. His finger ran down the lines of whatever was written in the book.

Ned coughed, but Whitmore continued to read, turning a page and placing his finger at the top of the next page and drawing it down again.

Ned swallowed and coughed again.

"This is not an apothecary." Whitmore's voice was a harsh whisper.

"S...sorry."

"I have no cure for yar cough," Whitmore said, his eyes still following his finger down the page. He scratched at the end of his grey stubbled chin.

"I don't have a cough."

"Then shut up." Whitmore coughed.

"I-I...have something to sell."

Whitmore looked up from his book, his dark eyes studying Ned. "Well?"

Ned walked until he was against the desk, waiting until then to draw out the gold chain, keeping it close to him.

Whitmore reached for the chain.

Ned drew it back.

"I need to see it."

Ned, reluctant, lowered the chain into Whitmore's outstretched hand, finally letting go of the pendant. He flinched as Whitmore's bony hand clenched around the chain.

Whitmore drew the chain to himself before uncurling his fingers enough to scrutinise Ned's pay.

"What's the pendant?" Whitmore asked.

"I-Ink."

"Horrible thing. Keep it." Whitmore continued to scrutinise the chain, prodding it every so often.

"But the chain?"

"It's a good one, innit." Whitmore stroked the chain between his index finger and thumb. "But too good for me."

"What?"

"Too good. Not 'nough money to pay ya for that."

"What?" *Too good. How can —? He's got to have the money.*

"I don' have the money to give ya."

Ned's mind tumbled over what Whitmore had said, trying to find some comprehension. "Ya must."

"Must I?" Whitmore looked at him again, his dark eyes hard, his lips twisted into a snarl. "'Larks seem to think we have to buy everything. That we're made of shillings and sovereigns. But sorry. We ain't. A Broker has money troubles just as much as ya. And sorry, a piece fine as this, I don't have the money to give ya honest price. Ya could take ya pick of my stock."

No. No. "Ya stock's not goin' ta feed me." *And it won't buy me a poultice.* "I'll try somewhere else." He could. He could go to another broker. Keep on going until he found someone with the money. If it was as good as Whitmore said, he'd find someone.

Whitmore's snarl had turned into a smirk. "Ya could. Ya could. But they don't know ya. They don't know ya're a 'lark. They'll call the

'Spectorate. And the Inspectorate won't listen. They'll have ya for theft, and ya'll be dancing a jig in Sullivan's Court Square. Least yar corpse might make some money for the hangman."

"Someone'll believe I found it."

"Why should they? Listen. They'll either short change ya on the sale. Or they'll tell the coppers to get in good with them, so coppers won't see what else the broker's up to."

"But..." Ned's voice drifted off as Whitmore shook his head. *There has to be a way. I can't find something this good. And...And...Be this close. This close to money and —*

His thoughts were cut-off by Whitmore tilting his head. "O' course," Whitmore said without going on.

"What?"

Whitmore continued to contemplate whatever thought had struck him.

"What?"

"There is a way we could do this deal."

Ned leaned in. "How?"

"We agree a price and I promise ta pay ya it once I've sold the chain."

"I leave it with ya?"

Whitmore glared at him. "Yes. How else am I to sell it?"

"But how do I know ya'll pay?"

"'Cause I promise."

"No proof, though, to the agreement."

Whitmore searched his desk, drawing out a pen from beneath the book. He scrutinised the pendant, working out how to open it and, once it was opened, he dipped the pen in. He turned his book to a blank page and began to scratch down letters.

"What ya doing?" Ned asked.

"Promissory. Ya read?"

"'Nough."

Whitmore gave a coughing laugh. "Good. Ya'll know I'm not screwing ya. It says I promise to pay a sovereign on sale of this chain."

He's screwing me. "And what if ya don't?"

Whitmore didn't respond.

"What if ya don't?"

"It's a promissory. I promise to pay, and I keep to it."

"What if ya don't?" Ned gripped at the desk.

"What would ya like to happen? My nose to grow? My teeth to rot? Ya've lost out there. Maybe my heart to stop."

"Yes."

Whitmore snarled as he dipped the pen back into the ink.

"Go on. Write it."

"Or?"

"Or ya don't get the chain."

The smirk returned to Whitmore's lips. He continued to write. "If that's what ya wish."

He signed the bottom of the page and offered the pen to Ned. Ned dipped it in the pendant's ink and scratched his name in unsteady letters.

Once done, Whitmore tore the sheet from the book and set it with a bundle of papers.

Ned's shack
Mudlarks' Way, Southport district

Ned flexed his arm, gritting his teeth against the lancing pain. The infection had been long in coming, but now his arm was swollen and pus soaked the bandage. He was glad that the stench of the river was hiding the smell of his flesh. Any hope of getting a poultice for his wounds lay with Whitmore selling the chain.

As the infection had set in, Ned's tolerance for being out on the riverbeds had dwindled and in the past day a sheen of sweat had covered his body. He needed the money, otherwise his blood would poison him or he'd starve to death.

As the pain relaxed to a dull throb, Ned pulled his coat around him and forced himself through the door of the shack.

He shivered as the sharp air cut through his clothes and the sweat. His hand went to the door ready to return to his bed, his mind arguing that maybe he'd be in a better shape in a few hours or a day. But he forced himself on.

He huddled into himself, trying to keep his body from touching anyone else as his heavy feet carried him through the crowded streets towards Everett's Green.

By the time he reached Whitmore's shop, his legs quaked. He licked the thick saliva from around his gums and entered.

Whitmore's eyes were fixed on his damn ledgers.

"I've come for my money," Ned said. *Don't let him get away.*

"I have no money for ya."

"Then give me the chain."

Whitmore looked up. "What chain?"

Ned's mind froze. "The chain I gave ya to sell." His voice was weak, thready. He needed to sound stronger. He tried again: "The chain I gave ya to sell." His voice was still weak.

"Ya're mistaken," Whitmore said as his attention went back to his books.

"No." Ned thumped the hand of his good arm down onto the table.

"Ya're."

Why's he doin' this? "I came here. Ya wrote a promissory."

"There's no promissory." Whitmore sounded so sure, his attention still held by the books and his finger going down the columns.

"Ya wrote it. For a gold chain. 'I promise' for the money ya'd get for it."

"Ya can check the ledgers."

"If y'ain't sold it, then give it back." Some strength had returned to his voice.

"Ya won't find yar…What was it?…A —"

"Gold chain."

"Gold? From the likes of ya?" Whitmore gave a coughing laugh.

"Don' laugh." Ned's voice was weak again, barely a whisper. His face, already hot from the poison in his blood, burned.

"Look for it. If ya find it, ya can take it."

Ned stood staring at Whitmore, then turned, his eyes darting amongst the piles of bric-a-brac that cluttered the shop. He reached behind a pile of sheets, felt in pots and pans. Nothing.

He tore at the shop with good arm and bad, pulling brushes and clothes from where they rested. It had to be there. He had to find it.

Whitmore looked up at Ned as his stock clattered to the ground. "Break it and ya pay."

It was enough.

Ned fled the shop.

How? How the…Damn him to Mhal's realm and let maggots eat his cock. The bastard…

The Sini River, Southport district

That night, Ned forced himself out on to the riverbed. He found nothing and by the end of the night he could barely stand from the shivering that wracked his body.

By the time he'd arrived back in his shack, he had resolved to return to Whitmore the next day. He would force him to pay the money.

Plowham Road, Everett's Green district

Ned's thumb stroked the dulled edge of the knife blade. He could feel the eyes of the people walking the street burning into him. *Someone'll see. Can't do this. Can't...*

He pushed open the door.

The stench of shit filled his nose.

He held his breath as he stumbled forward. *Don't worry 'bout it. Keep the knife ready to stick it in his throat. Just keep...keep...*

The thoughts ran from his mind.

Whitmore sat on his chair, slumped back, blank eyes staring at the ceiling, one hand clutched to his chest, gripping hard to his coat.

Shit. Shit.

"Whitmore?" The word was a whisper. "Whitmore." Stronger this time.

Whitmore didn't respond.

Get the Watch. Run. Go.

Ned shuffled forward, hand involuntarily reaching for Whitmore. The stench grew with each step. "Whitmore?"

Whitmore didn't move.

He's dead.

Ned touched his face, recoiling from the cool flesh.

He's dead.

Run. Get the Watch.

Bastard. Bastard.

Ned's hand reached for his knife, clenching round the wooden handle.

Bastard. Dying before...

The knife was out of his pocket, ready to be thrust forward.

Bastard.

The money. He'll have money.

He put the knife back, his eyes searching the room.

He moved quickly now, forcing his legs on faster and faster as he searched, looking for where Whitmore would have kept his money.

It was at the back of the room. A small lockbox on a desk, secured with a padlock.

Ned returned to the body. He searched the table, then, steeling himself, he searched Whitmore's pockets.

Nothing.

Has to be somewhere. He'd keep it close.

Ned ran his hands down Whitmore's body, feeling for the key. He pried Whitmore's hand away from his chest. And there was the bump.

Ned undid the shirt to reveal a key on a leather thong.

He lifted the key up over Whitmore's head and then stumbled towards the lockbox. He fumbled with the lock and key, until there was a click. He lifted the lid.

The coins were just dull disks in the gloom, nothing to distinguish copper from silver or — if he were lucky — gold.

He pulled the coins out in handfuls, stuffing them into his pockets, hoping they wouldn't seep through the holes. As his pockets filled, he searched around for other things to hold his horde. A satchel hung from the corner of a shelf. He grabbed it.

Once the lockbox was emptied, he hurried away, not looking back, not stopping until he was at his shack.

He stared at the slatted wooden walls and then burst into tears.

Ned's shack
Mudlarks' Way, Southport district

Ned had bought a poultice, had his arm treated and eaten a good meal at a tavern before he even thought to count how much coin he had taken. There had been no gold, but the shillings, pence and farthings had added up, and he'd been left with a sovereign, eleven shillings and four pence. A fortune.

A fortune he had soon realised he couldn't spend.

It was fine perhaps to spend a little here and there on better food, he may even have been able to get away with buying some warmer clothes and better boots. But if he were to find a better place to live then he would have to be careful, spending too much too soon would raise suspicions.

There was also the other issue — how to protect his fortune. He had thought to put it all in his bank. But that seemed foolish; there was always the risk that it could be found, no matter how slim that chance might be. Keeping it on his person or in his shack was worse. So he had decided to split it between all three — a large share in the bank and smaller shares in his shack, pockets and, once he'd bought a new pair, his boots.

He'd made a show of going out onto the riverbed each night, making sure no one had reason to suspect something had changed with him. Each night he came back with nothing, not that he cared, his mind too distracted by thoughts of his luck to search. With each night, though, a thought had snuck in: *I've been found out. Someone knows. Someone will find me and I'll get arrested for his murder.*

He was asleep when the knock came, the clatter against the door breaking through the fog of unconsciousness. His hand drew the knife from beneath the pillow before he'd even worked out what the noise meant.

A Divided River

Ned wiped the sleep from his eyes, the insistent knocking still drumming through his skull. Coat and boots on, he shuffled to the door and peered through a crack in the boards.

The knocking stopped. The man the other side rummaged in a leather satchel and drew out a copper coin, holding it out to Ned's eye.

The comte's face was embossed on the metal, 'Everett's Green' written around the top edge and 'In Service to the City' written around the bottom.

Ned's throat tightened, strangling his breath. It was an inspector from Everett's Green.

"Open up."

Ned hurried to hide the knife in his pocket.

"Open up. Sergeant Bartlett of Everett's Green Inspectorate."

Ned fumbled with the lock and opened the door.

Bartlett entered, moving past the silent Ned. The sergeant looked around the bare shack before turning his attention back to Ned. "Ya're a 'lark?"

Ned nodded, using all his thought to stop himself trembling.

"Where'd'ya sell your..." Bartlett was searching for the word.

Pay. Pay. Ned remained silent, just staring at Bartlett.

"Pay? That what ya call it?"

Ned nodded.

"Where'd'ya sell it?"

"Brokers." Ned's voice was thin, reedy.

"Any p'ticular?"

He knows. He... What do I say? Ned shrugged.

"Ever sold to Whitmore on Plowham Road?"

Ned's jaw tensed, his hand fumbled into his pocket, feeling for the knife. *Don'. Don' be stupid. Tell the truth. Can't do anything else...But...* He nodded.

"See, Mister Whitmore's been found dead —"

"I didn' kill him."

Bartlett tilted his head, puzzled.

What've I said?

"Died of natural causes. Best we can tell, his heart gave out."

"Then why're ya here?"

"Money's gone missing."

"Noth—" Ned coughed, freeing the phlegm that had choked his words. "Nothing to do with me."

"Maybe not. 'Cept we found a promissory. Sovereign's quite a bit to be owed."

"And he paid."

Bartlett furrowed his brow, his eyes staring into Ned's.

Ned tightened his body, trying not to tremble. Trying not to show fear.

Bartlett walked to the door. "Maybe he did."

"He did."

Bartlett didn't seem to hear as he opened the door.

"He did."

But Bartlett had left.

The Wheel and Horse
Horseman's Way, Trader's Gate district

His heart gave.

But...

Ned pulled another chunk of meat from the cooked chicken.

He wrote it, and it happened.

He sat next to the fire of the Wheel and Horse, enjoying the warmth, food and beer. Since the sergeant had appeared, Ned had spent as much time as possible away from Mudlarks' Way, hiding amongst the crowds of merchants and visitors in Trader's Gate.

Ya can't write things and make 'em happen.

He tore more meat from the chicken and bit chunks from it.

Too much a coincidence.

But he died.

But he must of written lots of things. What's different this time? Why would h—

Ned coughed as the chicken caught in his throat. He coughed again and spat the chunk of white flesh back onto his plate.

He used my ink.

He used…

But that was ridiculous, he chided himself. *How can ink make things happen?*

I could test it. If it's true, I could test and then…

He tried not to think beyond this, tried to concentrate on how he could test the ink's abilities.

The girl's grim face strained with thought as she read the paper in her hands, every so often casting glances at the Wheel and Horse's patrons packed around them, jostling for position in the overcrowded inn. It was a simple agreement: she would pool her efforts as a mudlark with him and they would share the profits, each taking a third of the profit of the other. It was a heard of agreement amongst the 'larks, a way of ensuring a little continuity of income. However, inevitably, both sides attempted to hide their true profits from the others within the agreement.

"Ya understand it?" Ned asked.

The girl looked up, fearful for a moment before giving a sharp nod.

He held out the pen.

She grasped it, uncertain, staring at the wooden implement, the ink threatening to drip from the nib.

Sign it, ya bloody... He'd been kind. He saw no point in punishing the girl unfairly. It said that if she didn't pay a third of her pay every Sunanday she would lose her hair. He hadn't said how. He hoped she'd think it would be him clipping her and selling the hair to cover the losses. But Ned hoped it would fall out, like Whitmore's heart had failed him.

The girl's knuckles whitened with the strength of her grip on the pen as she scratched out an M and E and something that could have been a G.

He took the paper and pen. "See ya Sunanday." He didn't look at the girl as he left, pushing past the other patrons, wanting to get to the open air.

Ned's shack
Mudlarks' Way, Southport district

The rattle of the door thundered through his sleep-fogged mind.

"Ned...Ned!" A voice, vaguely familiar, called out.

Ned's hand scrambled for the knife beneath his pillow.

"Ned!"

Shit...Shit... His mind scrambled trying to remember whose voice it was. He knew it was bad. Someone he didn't want to see. *Shit...Sergeant...Bartlett. The sergeant. Shit.*

He hid the knife in his coat pocket as he hurried to the door. He peered through a crack at the sergeant.

"Ned. I need ya to open up."

Ned undid the lock and chain. "What can I do for ya?" He asked, trying to keep the nerves from his voice.

"I need to ask some more questions," Bartlett said as he entered the shack. He was pulling out a bundle of papers as he did.

"What ones?" Ned asked as Bartlett looked about the shack before finding a small chest on which to rest the papers.

"What?" Bartlett sat on the bed and lifted the small chest onto his lap.

"What questions?

"Ya said ya had a promissory?"

Ned nodded as Bartlett pulled a stubby pencil from a pocket and started to write on the paper.

"And it was with Whitmore for a sovereign in advance of him selling a necklace?"

Ned nodded again. Bartlett scribbled.

"And he paid?"

"Yes." Ned tried to keep his face straight so as not to betray the lie.

"And he paid when?"

"'Bout a week ago." *When'd he die? Which day?*

"Do ya know which day?"

"I-I-" Bartlett's eyes narrowed, scrutinising Ned. "I think it was..." *Kinday?* "Quarday."

Bartlett scribbled. "And he was well enough when ya left him?"

Ned nodded.

"D'ya know of any 'larks that use the place other than ya?"

Ned shook his head. It wasn't a lie.

"And ya didn't take anything else from the shop, other than what was owed t'ya?"

Ned shook his head again.

Bartlett continued to scribble, his writing hurried. The point to his pencil snapped. He looked at the pencil in disgust and threw it at a wall. "Ya got anything to write with?"

"Yes," Ned said before he could stop himself.

"Well, can I have it?"

Slowly, Ned made his way to his coat and pulled out a pen and the ink. They were heavy in his hand. *He'll ask. He'll ask where I got them.*

He handed them to Bartlett.

Bartlett dipped the pen in the ink and scribbled a few sentences before turning the paper towards Ned. "Can ya sign ya name?"

"What?" Ned's eyes stared at the offered pen.

"Sign ya name? Or make ya mark?"

"What? Why?" Ned's throat tightened. He coughed.

"As ya're a suspect, I need ya to sign it to say its yar statement."

"I'm —" His constricted throat cut off his words. "I'm a suspect?"

"Ya didn't think ya were?" Bartlett chuckled.

"And if I don'?"

"Ya'll be held a liar and arrested for the crime."

Ned took the pen and inscribed his name.

The Wheel and Horse
Horseman's Way, Trader's Gate district

The girl slid the copper ha'penny across the table to Ned.

"That it?" Ned asked as he slid across the two pennies he owed the girl.

The girl nodded before grabbing the coins and rushing from the table.

Good. She lied.

The Merchant's Rest
The Turnpike, Trader's Gate district

The girl hadn't appeared for their second meeting. He had started his search on the streets of Trader's Gate, where he'd first found her. He'd tried not to have to pay for information, but in the end he'd had to hand over a few pence to find out where she slept.

He would lose a night out on the riverbed, but if he could prove his theory it wouldn't matter. He waited across the Turnpike at the Merchant's Rest, watching the Black Horse Inn until the lights started going out.

Ned slipped out into the rain-soaked street. The Turnpike was empty, the last of the merchants having settled in their inns for the night.

He hurried across the cobbles, heading for the alley that ran along the Black Horse's stable walls. Flat against the wall, he listened for movement in the stable yard.

Nothing.

Ned looked to the end of the alleyway, staring through the dark and downpour, to check that no one was passing by and then grabbed at the wall, using the stonework to gain purchase and climb over the wall.

He dropped into the courtyard beyond. The Black Horse was a rambling set of interconnected buildings. The original inn was to his right, with what may have once been a house to his left, the two buildings connected at the first floor. He passed beneath the bridging rooms, huddling into his coat and pulling his cap down. He slowed his breathing so as not to deafen himself to his surroundings.

Amongst the patter of rain came the creak of a door.

Ned stumbled towards a wall, hoping the shadows would hide him from whoever walked through the door.

Act like ya supposed to be here.

He forced himself away from the wall, walking on, head bowed, trying to reassure himself that if he just acted as though he was a guest, whoever came through the door wouldn't challenge him.

He nearly stumbled back to the shadows when he saw the light spilling out from the doorway. A man stood there, backlit, a wisp of smoke drifting up above his head.

The figure seemed to nod.

Ned managed a nod back and hurried on towards the stable door.

His hand rested on the handle.

Don't look back.

Could he be so sure that the figure in the door wasn't watching him? That the figure wasn't just going to rush him and beat him? His hand drifted into his pocket to feel his knife.

He opened the door to the smell of damp horse and straw.

The barest of light lit the stalls and the vague outlines of the horses. Amongst the snorts and grunts of the horses came snores. It seemed that more people than the girl used the stables on a night.

He crept along, peering into the stalls as he went.

She was midway down, curled into the hay that lined the flagstone floor. Her arm was curled over her head, obscuring sight of her hair.

The stall door creaked as Ned opened it.

The girl stirred but didn't wake, muttering to herself as she settled back into the hay.

Ned crept forward, peering through the darkness, trying to make out whether there was any hair on her head.

The girl was wearing a cap.

He knelt down, trying to work out some way to lift the hat and gain sight of her hopefully bare head.

The girl's arm twitched, then slid, curling up against her body.
Ned pulled gently at the cap. It tumbled from the girl.
What little hair remained was brittle.

The Sini River, Southport district

Ned had not slept since seeing the girl's head. He'd caused her hair to fall out. He had written it, and it had fallen out. But the question now was how he could make use of the ink. What he needed was for people to keep their promises, not for them to be punished for not keeping them.

As light had appeared in the gaps in his shack's walls, Ned had left to walk along the riverbank.

The air was damp and cool on his skin as he watched the ships drift in and out of port.

He could only think of one idea. He would need to create a contract that would cost the person breaking it money. But what contract and who?

He continued to watch the ships and boats rock on the waves of the changing tide.

Water Street, Trader's Gate district

Ricks lifted the girl from her feet, his slab of a hand tightening around her throat. The girl thrashed at his thick arm, trying to break the hold as her pale face turned red.

"Have ya got the pay?" Ned asked.

The girl gurgled as she shook her head.

"Ya lost your hair. Ya found something and didn't pay."

The girl pulled at Ricks's arm, her nails drawing red marks along his skin.

"Let her down."

Ricks opened his hand and the girl dropped, staggering as she found her feet.

She let out a choking splutter, sucking in gulps of air.

Ned had hired Ricks on the dockside. A simple transaction of a couple of pence a day, a signature of sorts and Ricks would protect him from any injury or sacrifice his pay for that day.

The girl felt in a pocket of her coat and threw a handful of coins at him as she continued to retch and splutter, phlegm streaming from her mouth to the earthen ground of the alleyway.

Ned bent and collected the coins, handing two pennies over to Ricks for his pay. Ricks placed his money in a coat pocket.

"How —" The girl was cut off by a coughing fit. "How'd ya make it fall out?"

Ned could feel his face flush. He struggled to keep looking at her, so turned away and walked from the alley. He tried not to think about the girl.

Ricks followed, overtaking him.

Ned felt in his pocket for the blade of his knife. He slid his thumb along the blade, letting it slit the flesh. He winced and drew his hand out of his pocket sucking on the trickle of blood.

As he followed Ricks, he noticed two copper pennies on the ground.

Ned fetched up the coins and pocketed them.

The Wheel and Horse
Horseman's Way, Trader's Gate district

"Ya saying to me that I give ya first pick and ya have to buy it?" Jude asked, a bemused smirk creasing his already lined face.

Ned nodded. Jude was the fifth to be offered the deal. He'd had to sweeten it the first time with the promise to buy something. "And if ya don't, ya sacrifice all ya worth and goods," Ned said.

Jude shook his head, the smile broadening until he saw the glare on Ricks's face

It was a simple plan. At least Ned hoped it was simple. He had money, he could set himself up in business as a broker. The problem was having 'larks sell him their pay. Most already had good deals with brokers, but, if he could get the best of their pay, he hoped he could set himself up in business as a middle man — collecting the items from the riverside and taking the risk of storing them until they could be sold on.

"Give me the pen," Jude said, holding out his hand.

Ned handed it to him. The ink from the pendant was nearly all used, just enough for a signature or two more. But if it worked with the five 'larks that would be enough.

Jude scratched his signature and rose from his chair. With a glance at Ricks, he walked away. "See ya tonight and bring ya money."

Pen Street, Everett's Green district

Ricks slapped at his coat as he whirled around, searching the floor for his lost coins, his lips scowling.

Ned rubbed at the hand he'd knocked on a doorpost as he'd left the Wheel and Horse an hour ago. The jolt of pain had faded in minutes, but it had been enough for Ricks's coins to drop from his pockets and for Ned to collect them. He'd almost handed them back to Ricks. He hadn't intended to take them, but given the number of times that Ricks had lost his coins over the past weeks, if Ned had given them back Ricks would have realised something was wrong. He had, though, started to pay for Ricks's food whenever he could, otherwise his protection would have starved to death.

Giving in on finding his lost coins, Ricks threw a sack over his shoulder and stormed off down the narrow road. The sack contained the pay they'd be looking to sell today. Things were going well, each night provided a healthy haul of new items from his 'larks. With Ricks in his employ and the purchase of a good strongbox, he'd started keeping the pay and his earnings at his shack. He was hoping soon that he'd be able to leave the shack behind and start to live at an inn in Everett's Green or maybe even the Wheel and Horse.

Ned hurried after Ricks, trying to catch up with his long strides.

Pain flared in the back of his knee. He stumbled forward, lost his balance and fell to all fours with a yelp.

He could see Ricks turn as Ned tried to force himself back to his feet. But his aching leg went from him.

"Bastard. Where's my 'air? Where's my 'air?" Small fists pounded at his back.

He tried to reach round to grab the girl.

"Bastard. Bastard." The blows continued to rain down.

Ricks lumbered back towards him.

Already the others using the street had scattered away, hiding in doorways, trying not to see what would happen.

The girl was lifted off him, flung to one side.

She struck the wall of a house with the sound of snapping bone and slumped down.

Ricks helped Ned to his feet.

Ned's knee roared with pain each time he tried to put pressure on the leg. He let Ricks help him hobble along.

Ned looked back to see the rock that had struck him lying in the earth. The girl was still slumped against the wall, her eyes open, a whimper escaping her mouth.

Slowly, people returned to the street.

The Sini River, Southport district

The pay had been sold, and he'd had his leg tended to with some of the money. He'd needed to buy a stick to help him walk, but otherwise his wound would heal with time. It had cut into his profits.

He and Ricks stood watching the lights of the mudlarks fishing for pay amongst the mud and pools of water. Another hour and his 'larks would start coming to him with their offers. Ricks took a bite of a biscuit, crunching it, crumbs spilling from his mouth.

Ned had brought him a half-dozen biscuits to make up for the lost pay and given him a three-penny piece as a thank ya for his help with the girl. In some ways Ricks was lucky that Ned had been attacked when he had. He'd have lost two days pay if the girl had waited until the next day.

A 'lark's light was making it's way down the mud towards where they stood on the bank. It was too early for a 'lark to be coming to sell.

The light turned into the shape of a man and then the man was beneath them, climbing the ladder to the bank top.

As the figure reached the top, the light was enough to show the man's face — Jude.

Ricks brushed the crumbs from his clothes and straightened, bringing his size to bear as Jude approached.

"Ya early?" Ned said, still surprised that a 'lark would be coming off the mud so soon.

Jude didn't respond, just kept walking towards them.

Ricks moved forward, placing himself in front of Ned.

"What ya got?"

Jude didn't respond, just coming to a stop in front of Ricks.

He pulled something from his pocket.

The line of gold twinkled in the lantern light.

"Ya'll buy it?" Jude asked.

Before he could think, Ned nodded. "A sovereign."

"Ya got that sort of money?"

"I can get it." He'd need to go back to his strongbox and maybe take a little from the original coin he'd stashed at his bank, but he could make it, and he was sure he could sell it on. Even if he had to find a jeweller himself. He'd make money, more than the gold he'd hand over to Jude.

Jude set his lamp on the ground and held out his hand, ready for his pay.

"Give me an hour."

"Someone'll notice me stood here for that long. They'll come and have my pay."

Ned pulled out what coins he had on him and thrust them at Jude. "Here's some now. Ya go and find yourself a nice safe place for a while, and we'll be back in an hour."

Jude smiled and took the coin.

Baker Row, Everett's Green district

There had been a little less money in the strongbox than he'd hoped, but Ned knew there was more than enough at his bank. He'd had to hope that Jude would wait the extra time it would take for Ned to get to Everett's Green and back.

His fingers searched along the beam for the familiar feel of the leather satchel strap. It wasn't there.

Had he moved it? It had been some time since he'd last checked the satchel; well before his last visit from Bartlett. But it should have been safe. He didn't always return it to the same place.

He moved along the side of the building, reaching up again to feel along the beam.

Nothing.

He moved again.

Ricks stood staring at him.

Shit. Shit. It's gone. "Get here and search."

Ricks joined him against the building and started running his hands along the beam. Ned headed in the opposite direction.

Once at the end of the building they turned.

"Ya sure this is the right one?" Ricks asked.

"Yeh." Ned's voice was strangled by his growing dread.

"Someone's stolen it."

I've already given him some money. If I don't give him everything he gets the money and the chain. I need...I need. I need more money. But...

He felt in his pocket for his knife, letting it slit his thumb.

Ned walked towards Ricks.

"Ya cut your thumb," Ricks said as Ned neared.

"Just a nick. Ya go first." Ned nodded towards the entrance to the alley.

"What ya gonna do without the money?"

"I don't know." Ned crouched to scoop up the three-penny piece that had fallen from Ricks. As he straightened he saw that Ricks had stopped and turned to him.

Ricks looked at the coin in Ned's hand before checking his pockets. "Mi—" He stopped, his jaw dropping in realisation.

Ned tried to duck as Ricks's hand flew round, but he was too slow, the fist connecting hard with his jaw. There was a crack, and his face flared in agony.

Ned staggered back, bringing his arms up to defend himself.

But it was pointless, each blow sent pain lancing through his body. His vision blurred. He tried to stand, but the punches drove him to his knees and then flat to the ground.

Blood trickled down Ned's throat. His vision darkened. Pain was the only sensation. He blacked out.

Bartlett crouched down beside the body. It was broken and twisted, the limbs pointing at angles that shouldn't have been possible if the man was alive. He rolled the body over. The face was black from bruising, its lips crusted with mud and blood.

It was Ned.

Bartlett stood, cracking his tense neck, before returning his tricorn to his head. He sighed. With Ned dead it meant perhaps they'd never close the case on the theft from Whitmore. And now he had Ned's murder to investigate.

An amused huff escaped his nose as he remembered the statement Ned had signed.

May justice find me if I have lied.

Maybe he'd lied.

A Divided River

ON THIS DAY, the Twelfth of Mensesis, aetate lux 69,

I, THOMAS EVERETT, Comte de Vasini, by the will of my seigneurs, and under the scrutiny of the Médiateurs de la Ville, hereby write and seal into **THE LAW OF VASINI** the following:

In accordance with THE FIRST of our FOUNDING LAWS, which prohibits the worship of the deities that have fallen, the tattooing of parts of the body, whether human or not, with ink, as was done in worshipping the goddess Rasah, shall be deemed abhorrent and punishable under the law.

This law shall specify the following areas of the body that shall not bear a tattoo on threat of punishment: the face; any portion of the throat that lies between the space of the neck from one earlobe to the other (or where an earlobe should be in a full and complete human); the left side, from the perspective of the person tattooed, and centre of the front of the chest that runs from clavicle to the last rib; the genitalia and the place above the genitalia where hair may grow; the buttocks.

Should a person be found to bear a tattoo in such a location, **it is decreed that the following punishments shall be mete out:**

If the tattoo is found not to have been inscribed for the worship of RASAH, the tattoo shall be burnt from the flesh so that it no longer remains. A tenth of the wealth of the convicted individual shall be forfeited to the city.

If, however, the tattoo is found to have been inscribed for the worship of RASAH, then the convicted has broken the First Founding Law, and shall be presented in at least three public squares for the citizenry of Vasini to see the face of the convicted. At each square, the convicted's crimes shall be read to the assembled citizenry and the convicted shall be flogged with a twig of birch for a number of strokes that shall be determined by the judge who passes judgement on the convicted with good mind to the severity of the crime. The convicted shall then be taken to a place of public execution where their crimes shall be read once more and there they shall be hanged till near death, whereupon they shall be cut from beneath the sternum to genitalia, their intestines removed and roasted upon coals. Once dead, they shall be cut into four and one part shall be taken to each square in which their crimes were read — to include where they were executed — and there **displayed for seven days as a warning to those who would worship the deities and threaten our freedom.** The body may then be sold and the monies given to the gaol as payment for the imprisonment and punishment of the condemned.

THE WINTER FAYRE

I

Palace Bridge
The Down Hibourne ditch, Palace district

Kemp watched the wisps of his breath billow out before him. His mother would have called it 'Khordra's breath'.

On the ice river below, the first stalls were being erected by lamplight. A chestnut seller walked between them handing out his wares. It wouldn't be too long until the frozen Hibourne ditches and Sini River would be covered with the city's people, excitement and enjoyment driving the cold from their bones.

Kemp gathered snow from the bridge's rail and pounded it between his gloved hands until it was a rough ball and flung it out onto the river. It struck a patch of ice that had been swept clear of snow and split, scattering.

Kemp picked up his musket and continued his patrol on from the Palace Regiment barracks towards the Palace itself, looking forward to a mug of mulled wine at the Palace kitchens.

Runt Street, Southgate district

Hat's thin legs gathered pace despite her mind telling them not to run. It had seemed like the entire city was whispering "There's a winter fayre. The comte has called it. The Winter Fayre's here." She'd fled the house before even the Barker had risen, woken as she had been by the whispering through the walls.

The snow hadn't come into the streets, the buildings too tight together, but the ground was still hard with frost and it hurt her feet to walk so fast. She wrapped her coat tighter around her, its threadbare cloth barely enough to keep the cold from her flesh, but four layers of shirts and woollen waistcoats made the air bearable. And there'd be fires at the Fayre. She'd worn fingerless gloves, all the better for her trade.

Thoughts of the fat purses and the hot food flickered through her head, her lips creeping into a smile.

Palais de Vasini, Palace district

The snow glistened pink in the dawn light as the city's servants huddled up the steps into the Palace. Alfred Burston prodded an underling from his path with his cane. The young woman turned to glare but realised whose cane it was and dropped her head to watch her feet again, moving to the side to let Burston through.

Burston swerved past her, taking firm steps despite the ice, and came to a stop. A man he didn't recognise stood before him, head bowed, unwilling to move forward. Burston readied his cane to jab again.

The mass of the city's servants was at a halt. Something must have blocked their ways.

Burston stretched up his neck, trying to see what irritant was causing the problem, but all he could see was a mass of heads and hats.

Burston brought his cane up, ready to jab, then heard the whispers. "The Fayre's been called."

Burston swivelled on his heels, steadying himself as he felt his feet nearly slipping. The idiot now before him hadn't turned. Burston's cane shot out and poked the tall man's shoulder.

The man didn't move.

Burston shoved harder. "That way." Burston forced himself past.

Timothy Everett's mansion
Founders' Way, Besson's Heights

Isaac refused to even touch the spoon that rested in his bowl of porridge. Timothy Everett had a wilful family. It pleased him in many ways but made some days unnecessarily torturous. Between mouthfuls of breakfast, his two daughters were discussing what they'd do at the Fayre, while Susan, Isaac's nanny, tried to coax the young boy to eat something to keep him warm for when he was outside. Anna, his wife, watched on as she drank coffee, trying to hide her amusement at her children's antics.

Timothy had his very own idea for the day. There was something — someone — he very much hoped to see. They would need to leave soon, though, if they were to make the most of the time before the Fayre was taken over by the ball games that inevitably descended into rucks and chaos and injuries.

"Please get Isaac dressed," Timothy told Susan as he rose from his seat. Susan looked up at him, blinking, trying to work out whether she could challenge the instruction.

Anna rose from her seat, her grin broadening. "Come now, girls. Let's get ready and we can talk tactics for a snowball skirmish." She held out her hands, and Amelia and Clara took them.

Timothy strode from the table, leaving Susan still blinking behind him.

The Down Hibourne ditch, Palace district

Claire warmed her hands on the bag of chestnuts, popping one into her mouth and crunching down. She stepped to one side to let a hurried bundle of children slip and slide their ways past. The Fayre had barely begun and already the frozen river was crowded. Everyone had become an amorphous bundle of coats, scarves and hats. All but the people of quality who, even in the harshness of winter, decided on style over practicality, their winter coats adorned with brocade, embroidery and fur, their wigs styled and balancing hats that served no use other than to carry feathers.

Claire watched the masses move past, blocking out the sounds of the stall holder and the chatter, trying to peer beyond the wrapped scarves to see the faces beneath. She hoped Jacob would come.

II

The Down Hibourne ditch, Palace district

Hat's fingers ran down the blade in her pocket — a handleless straight razor — as she followed the meandering line through the crowds. There was no hurry, apart from the children rushing between stalls, the adults seemed to enjoy the break from their everyday lives. They were so relaxed, so easy to target. The only difficulty was the clothing. Many would-be targets had buried their purses under various layers of coats and waistcoats. So far Hat'd been able to cut a purse and slip her fingers into the pockets of two others for a grand haul of five pence. She'd need to find a red or a blue to make her trip worthwhile. At least, though, she'd be able to buy some spiced buns and get a cup or two of mulled wine, maybe even go skeeting.

There was a flash of blue ahead, moving towards the riverbank where smoke rose from an ox roast. Hat sidestepped a fat man with a cane and moved back into the flow, keeping her eyes fixed on the sliver of blue ahead.

The blue stopped.

A series of blazing sticks appeared in the air — a juggler.

Hat hurried on, weaving amongst the crowd.

The blue stood watching the juggler with a dozen or so more people. A white wig balanced on the blue's head and cascaded down her shoulders. By what Hat could see of her face, the blue looked only a little older than her. Likely to be less cautious with her coin.

Hat walked on, letting her eyes drift off sideways to assess the woman's clothes — a tight blue woollen riding coat trimmed with fur over shirts and waistcoat, breeches and a fine belt, a velvet satchel over her shoulder, the bag stylishly small. She'd have a weapon, likely a stiletto, about her, but if Hat did it properly the blue wouldn't even notice.

Hat walked on past, merging with the crowd and slowly worked her way round to head back towards the juggler, who was coming to the end of his show.

It was all down to the timing. Hat slowed her footsteps, playing through her mind what was to come.

As the juggler added another two flaming sticks to his act, the crowd — and the blue — gasped. Hat slowed her steps further as she closed in.

The juggler flung the sticks out in rapid succession, the sticks impaling the snow at his spectators' feet.

The applause began, and the juggler tossed his cap down for coin.

And, yes, the blue turned to her satchel.

Hat hurried forward, keeping her head down.

If she'd timed it right, the blue would open the purse and toss a coin. She'd clap once more. Maybe shout a yay or bravo or whatever those from the Sovereigns said. And she'd be placing the purse back into the satchel and...

Hat struck the blue with her shoulder, the glancing blow of a careless girl in a rush. Hat's hand dipped in. "Sorry, Miss," Hat offered, her voice low.

She could feel the blue's glare, but Hat rushed on, not looking back. The purse was clutched in her hand, up inside her long coat sleeves. She put her hands into her pockets and lost herself in the crowd. She squished the velvet cloth, feeling the coins run together. Not many, but enough, especially if there was silver.

Burston's steps were slow across the ice. He was hesitant to lift his cane lest he lose his support. Groups of Scarlets and 'Fishers watched their children skeete round. The ice beyond the bridge between the Palace grounds and the Palace Regiment barracks was only accessible after paying a tariff, and, therefore, was the reserve of people of quality. Burston had managed to use his position to persuade the attendants that he was not required to pay the silver.

There was no sign of the Besson family amongst the groups of blue. Burston had hoped that maybe the city's most important family would want to be at the Fayre before it became too crowded and the ball games started. He looked amongst the groups, deciding from amongst the faces he could make out who would be best to approach first.

He settled on a group of Kingfishers, Emma Renard amongst them, watching their children skeeting across the ice, steaming mugs in their hands.

Burston continued his precarious walk towards a young man carrying a tray of mulled wine. He cast a coin on the tray and took a mug, carrying on to Emma Renard's group. A small collection of valets and maids stood back from their masters and mistresses, their red-cheeked faces set hard against the discomfort of the cold.

Burston approached the tallest valet, lifting his head and straightening his back. His feet nearly went from him. Burston planted his cane more firmly. "Alfred Burston. Baronnie des Bâtiments Publics et des Routes," Burston said.

The valet did not move, his eyes still looking to where his employer's children skeeted. A round of applause erupted from Emma Renard's companions, and the valet and other staff dutifully joined in. Burston, without even turning to see what had happened, clapped, careful not to spill his wine.

"Alfred Burston. Baronnie des Bâtiments Publics et des Routes," Burston said again.

The valet, still without meeting Burston's gaze, held out a gloved hand.

The insolence of the man, demanding money to introduce him. *But,* Burston thought as the flare of anger subsided, *if that is the price.* He yanked his purse from beneath his coat and selected a three-penny piece. He let the coin drop back into the purse and, on second thoughts, selected a half shilling.

The valet accepted the coin, making it disappear within his pockets, and, without even acknowledging Burston, walked to the side of his master — a willowy man, stood on the edges of Renard's group. The valet whispered in his master's ear. The master didn't respond. The valet whispered again. The master nodded.

The valet looked towards Burston, who took this as his cue. Careful now not slip or spill his wine, Burston took slow steps across the half-a-dozen yards to the willowy man, trying to remember the young 'Fisher's name.

Jeyne? Jeunet?

Burston's footsteps faltered, unable to settle on the correct name.

He needed to move, he couldn't appear to be reluctant, not after approaching him. Not if he were to gain audience with Renard.

"M-Monsieur." He had to take a risk. "Jeyne." He tried to keep the question from his voice.

"Mister Burston." The willowy 'Fisher said, not turning to face Burston, but offering his hand.

Burston shook the offered hand.

"This is not a day for business," Jeyne said.

"Of course not. I only looked to enquire whether you were enjoying the Fayre."

"My son and daughter are."

"They enjoy the skeeting?"

"You've never skeeted?"

Lie. "Yes. But when I was very young."

Jeyne raised his eyebrow.

The crowd clapped again as a blonde-haired girl rose one leg up behind her and glided along, the barest wobble in her stance. Burston joined in the clapping, nearly fumbling his mug.

Jeyne seemed to respond to some unseen gesture from Renard and moved across to the leader of the small pack of 'Fishers.

Burston cast his eyes to the skeeters as Jeyne and Renard exchanged whispers. He sipped from his mug, conscious of the other 'Fishers ignoring him.

Jeyne returned.

"You found your travel to the Fayre reasonable?" Burston asked.

"Yes," Jeyne said.

"And Madame Renard?"

"I am sure she did."

"We — my colleagues and I — have made extra efforts this year to keep the snows from the roads in Sovereign's Gate."

"I live in Temple Ruins."

"But-but the travel has been good?"

"Suitable."

"I shall see if we can make it good."

Burston waited for Jeyne to reply. Perhaps he hadn't heard. Surely Jeyne would thank him for the offer? Even as just a pleasantry?

Jeyne's silence continued.

Maybe if he spoke some more about the help he could provide. "Monsieur...I —"

"Burston, what do you think of my daughter's skeeting?" It was Renard. Renard was speaking to him.

Burston's heart beat in his throat, cutting off his speech. "I-I-I..."

"She is the one in the blue."

They were all wearing blue.

"I-I-I —" His throat cleared. "I believe her to be most excellent. You must be..."

One of the children tumbled to their backside. He hoped it wasn't Renard's daughter.

"...most proud of her."

"Not for her skeeting," Renard said. Her comment elicited slight laughs from her companions.

"She must have many qualities that make you proud."

"Like a diamond."

"A diamond?" Burston's cheeks flushed, embarrassed that he was already lost by her conversation. He hoped that it would be masked by the ruddiness brought on by the cold.

"Many sparkling facets," Renard said.

What was Renard trying to say? "Yes," Burston said.

"Is there anyone for more wine?" Jeyne asked.

"Yes," Burston said before he realised that the others had raised their mugs rather than state their need.

"Burston, if you would," Jeyne said handing Burston his mug.

Burston collected the mugs from the other 'Fishers, having to tuck his cane beneath his arm so as to hold all the mugs offered. He glanced at the valets and maids. They made no effort to come to his aid. *Damn them. Damn them to Mhal.* He chastised himself for thinking the god's name. A mug slipped from his little finger and plopped into the snow. *You're the staff, damn you. Not me. I'm...I'm...* He lowered himself to the ground and caught the mug's handle with a finger, slowly, creakingly rising to his feet again. *How dare you just stand there.* He tried not to glare at them.

Everett's eyes kept wandering to the passing masses, each look sending a quiver of anticipation through his stomach, hoping he would see her. Amelia and Clara skeeted with Richard, their eldest half-brother holding tight to them to keep steady, Richard's own children watching on from the bank with his wife, Beatrice. Susan and Isaac were off in search of food for the family, and Anna was searching for Everett's second eldest son, Robert.

Clara stumbled, her skeetes catching each other. She clung to her eldest brother, who held her tight, pulling her up before she could hit the ice.

Everett glanced away. They wouldn't miss him. He could walk off, just a little way and see if he could see her.

Clara looked at her father.

Look away. Concentrate on your skeeting.

Clara smiled.

Everett smiled back, waving. *Look away.*

Clara waved again. Amelia saw what her sister was doing and smiled and waved. Now Richard was looking at him.

Distracted, Amelia stumbled and fell, hitting the ice on her side.

Clara and Richard looked down at their sister, and Everett slipped away, wincing, a pang of guilt at leaving his fallen daughter. *She'll be fine*, he tried to reassure himself.

Everett could feel his hands tremble, despite the warmth of his gloves. He wanted to turn and look back at his son and daughters, but he knew he had to keep moving. His back felt bare. He was sure they were looking. Maybe just a glance to check that they hadn't seen.

But he forced himself on through the crowds.

The smell of roasting chestnuts reached him. He'd need to eat.

Everett paused by the chestnut seller, removing a glove so he could rummage in his pockets for a coin. He glanced back towards from where he'd come, but the crowds blocked all sight of his family.

He felt light headed with a resurgence of the guilt pang. Everett shut his eyes and asked for a bag of chestnuts.

Paying the seller he walked on, trying to force thoughts of his family from his mind while trying to work out where he would find the girl.

Kemp kept his head bowed as he walked amongst the stalls, casting glances to either side, watching people's hands as they dipped into pockets and pouches to find coin or keep warm. He had changed out of his uniform at the Palace. He now huddled into a black greatcoat like the ones the Manis traders wore, a woollen cap pulled down tight on his head. The pockets were deep enough to hide a pistol in each. He knew there would be at least twenty others from the Palace's Third Fusiliers hidden amongst the crowds, keeping an eye out for troublemakers.

It'd been the same since the troubles after Dame Emerson's murder. Any large gathering of the masses, and the Third were sent in dressed as civvies to keep an eye, make sure the Ranters didn't get too rowdy.

He watched face after face, trying to anticipate what each one was about to do, who they were, who they were meeting with, trying to see the clue that suggested something was wrong, something was different.

He strode on.

Music drifted amongst the chatter and calls. Someone was singing by an ox roast, an enrapt crowd circling the singer and his guitar.

Kemp let his feet carry him towards the music, humming in tune as he went.

The bag of chestnuts was gone, and Jacob still hadn't arrived. Claire had forced herself to remain where she was, knowing that trying to search amongst the masses would be fruitless and risk missing her meeting him. It was where she and Jacob had met for the past four years — the first day of the Winter Fayre, the east bank of the Down Hibourne ditch. They would meet and discuss what they should aim to do for the next year and then go their separate ways, no contact unless necessary to make sure if one of them was found they would not be able to betray the other.

The smell of the ox roast tempted her stomach with thoughts of warmth. She thrust her hands into her armpits, trying to keep them warm as she continued to stand and watch the faces of the passers by, trying not to let the nearby music distract her from her task.

She couldn't help but feel that something was not right. How would she know if it had gone wrong? She discarded the thought. Jacob's lateness could be due to any number of things. He could have succumbed to a bout of his illness and now could not make it to their meeting. He could have been delayed. He could yet to have heard the Fayre had been called. It was still early.

But she couldn't help but feel a sense of dread curl around her stomach.

"The old man dies, a child is born," the red-haired musician sang, strumming at his guitar. The singer sat entertaining the ox roast's patrons. *"As snow falls."*

More easy pickin's, Hat told herself as she meandered towards the roast. She had intended to just buy some food and move on, but the sight of such a captivated crowd was too tempting.

"The darkness swallows."

Hat slowed to take in the scene, trying to pick out the best targets, letting the music trickle in as she watched. There weren't any reds or blues, but there were some who looked well off enough.

A couple with their offspring were paying for their roast. The woman tucked her purse back inside her satchel.

"As fires burn."

A girl, maybe Hat's own age, but so much plumper, her meaty cheeks flushed red, tipped a coin into a box at the musician's feet.

"Lie by the hearth, wait for the morn."

The girl waddled to her father, nearly slipping. The father, as wide as the casks Hat'd seen rolled into the Gangman's Coin near Runt Street, took the girl's arm. His purse was still out. Hat started towards them but the man was too quick, tucking the purse inside his coat.

"Sleep, sleep."

But then a man came alongside them, hobbling along with a cane, heading for the ox roast. He was already reaching for his purse. It looked heavy.

"*Wait for the morn.*"

Hat fell into step behind the man with the cane, trying to keep the smile from her face.

He was too warm. He could feel sweat prickle along his back.

I'm not their servant. They. They should understand. I am a ranking Palace official. I can be a...good...a good ally. A good friend. But —

"*Let hearth and home keep you warm.*" The song cut through, momentarily breaking into Burston's thoughts.

Burston's lip curled in annoyance at the disruption. He forced himself on, trying to find somewhere to go.

The music and chatter and movement all around him continued to press in on his mind.

A man bumped his shoulder. A foot struck his cane. The smell of roasting ox played at his nose. A tug at his pocket.

Burston whirled, planting his cane down hard so as not to lose his footing. His hand flew out grabbing a wrist and twisting the arm up so he could see what the hand contained.

Everett strode forward before his mind even registered what he was doing. The girl needed help. She'd been caught. After the past three years, someone other than him had caught her. His foot kicked at the man's cane, sweeping it away. The man —

Everett recognised him from the Palace. The name was on his tongue.

— Tumbled, hitting the snow and ice hard, dragging the girl down with him.

The girl, thin as a twig, pulled her arm as hard as she could as she fell. Her other hand shot out, trying to steady herself, but only finding the man's —

What is his name?

— Face.

There was an oomph from the man, and then he was shouting at her. "You thief. You bogsman. You ditch shit."

The girl continued to try to pull away, but the man held hard.

Everett could see out of the corners of his eyes the crowd watching on, ripples of laughter joining the man's —

Burston!

— Insults.

Everett lunged, grabbing the girl round the waist and dragging her back, lending his weight to her struggle with Burston, his feet trying to find purchase in the snow.

The girl came free and Everett planted her on the snow, grabbing her arm.

She tried to pull away, but Everett was having none of it. He held tight and pulled her along with him as he hurried into the crowd.

Hat's feet nearly went from under her as she tried to dig them into the snow to stop the other man dragging her on. She scratched at his gloved hand, trying to force him to let go.

"Come on," the other man said without turning. "I'll get you somewhere safe."

All that filled Hat's head were images of the Watch dragging her away.

She forced her feet to stop, pulling back on her captured arm.

The other man halted.

"Come on," the other man said again.

"Let go," Hat said, pulling on her arm again.

"They'll arrest you." The other man's voice was hushed. He moved in close to Hat, the wisps of his breath joining with hers. He was fat under his thick coat. It looked like he'd never gone a day without food.

She pulled her arm. "Let me go."

The other man let go. "Do you trust me now."

Hat bolted forwards, pushing past the other man, shoving his soft belly out of the way.

The laughter still rang in his ears. *Useless braying donkeys. Cattle, the lot of them.* The Watch were nowhere to be seen. He'd write a letter to Gallieni, and maybe Fox, demand that they bring a punishment against Captain Finch for the lack of patrols. To not just be stolen from but to be assaulted, and by a man of at least some means by the glimpse of the man's black coat. The city needed a stronger hand.

Burston shuffled on through the crowd, eyes darting left and right, trying not to make contact with those around him but looking for his assailants. His arse, hip and leg ached and protested the movement, but he had to find them. If the Watch were to be useless to him, he'd bring the law to them himself.

The Sini River

Kemp had seen Burston turn on the thin girl — barely recognisable as a girl she was so thin and swaddled in layers of clothes — and then Everett had kicked the cane away. Why was a banker assaulting a servant of the city? And why was he helping a thief? It was strange and enough reason for Kemp to follow them as Everett pulled the protesting girl along with him as he fled the incident.

Everett hadn't stopped pulling until they were at the point where the ice of the Hibourne ditch met that of the Sini, the girl's protests finally getting the better of him. Once freed, the girl had stormed away, but Everett had not given in, following behind the girl out on to the ice amongst the stalls on the Sini.

Was Everett one of those rare-breed Ranters — a man of quality taken with the idea his inferiors deserved a greater say in the city? He'd never been spoken of as such when Captain Bell had taken them through all of the notable people to watch.

Kemp followed on, keeping a few people between himself and Everett, who kept his eyes locked on the girl. The girl tromped on, huddling into herself and casting baleful looks back at Everett as she wove in and out of the Fayre's visitors. She was heading for the Up Hibourne. It certainly seemed that this girl had no interest in Everett, despite the help he'd given. So why had Everett helped her? Kemp's mind ran through some options — *Favoured whore? Bastard child?* — but he discarded all of his thoughts as speculation.

The girl stopped inside the mouth of the Up Hibourne. Everett had said something, but, amongst the noise of the crowds, Kemp couldn't make out the words.

The girl turned and tromped back towards Everett. She stood rigid before him, sizing him up, arms crossed. The curl of her lip betrayed her mistrust.

Everett spoke again, and the girl's stance softened.

Kemp carried on towards them, hoping he would hear what they discussed.

Why is he helping her? The question had driven Claire to hurry after the man who had rescued the girl, her wait for Jacob momentarily forgotten. When thoughts of her fellow adherent had resurfaced, she was already some distance from the ox roast and it seemed pointless to return. *Just watch them for a little while to work out what's happening and then go back. Jacob can wait for a while.*

A man in a black greatcoat moved towards the girl and her rescuer. He had followed them, like Claire had, trying to look as though he was just part of the crowd, remaining several people back. A temptation flared within her to warn the girl and the rescuer, but she quelled it, chastising herself. She should only observe, not interfere. At least until she knew why the rescuer had intervened and why the man in the greatcoat was —

The girl's hand flew from her pocket, lashing out at her rescuer.

The rescuer, stumbled back, his feet going from him.

Light glinted off the blade in the girl's hand.

As her rescuer landed on his arse at her feet, the girl turned and ran.

The man who had followed them adjusted his path to follow the girl, quickening his pace but still trying to look as though he were just a part of the crowd.

Stay or run?
Why was he following her?
Why did she attack him?

Her eyes flashed between the rescuer, trying to force himself back to his feet, and the fast disappearing girl.

Claire was becoming paralysed by indecision.

Her feet hurried on, her eyes searching for glimpses of the girl amongst the drifting crowds.

Even if she didn't find out about the girl, maybe she could find out why the man in the greatcoat was following them.

Everett's feet lost purchase on the snow-covered ice, spilling him back onto his arse. With an exasperated sigh, he tried to find purchase again and levered himself to a crouch. Once sure of his footing, he straightened himself and looked for some sign of the girl.

Why had she attacked him? He'd tried to help. Burston would have had her arrested if he hadn't intervened.

He stumbled on, the movement uncomfortable with a sore backside. He felt at his face, tentative, expecting his gloved fingers to come away stained with blood. But there was nothing.

He couldn't see a thing amongst the crowds. He needed to get higher to see over them. He headed for the other bank, swerving amongst the steady stream of fayre goers. His hand went to guide someone from his path, but he pulled it back before it may contact with their arm.

Everett stepped up onto the bank. It only lifted him up two foot or so, but it was enough. He could see the tops of people's hats.

It wasn't her head he recognised. It was the movement. A hurry away from the Fayre, against the flow of people heading towards the stalls and entertainments.

There she was, a distance away, heading for the other bank, the flow of the masses between him and her.

Everett felt at his face, still expecting to feel blood. There was none.

He lowered himself back down to the ice river and pushed on towards the other bank.

It seemed as though everyone was determined to be in his way. A group of boys rushed ahead of their parents, ignoring the adults' calls for them to slow down. Girls, arm in arm, their eyes focused only on the other. An old man, himself trying to avoid a group talking as they bit into steaming bread-and-meats of beef and onion, the contents oozing from the sides. A group of children chasing each other, ducking snowballs and returning fire.

Everett scrambled onto the bank, his eyes searching. He turned, desperate for some sign of her, a glimpse of her hat, or the flutter of her coat, something.

There was noth —

The crowds on the bank parted for the briefest moment and there she was, running towards a street between the riverside houses. He rushed on.

Palace View, Eldereham district

There was a woman following the girl. The girl and Everett had yet to notice, but Kemp had seen her out of the corners of his eyes. The way she moved, the way she tried to keep behind him, suggested that she knew that he was following the girl as well. He slowed his steps, the woman overtook him, casting the slightest glance at him as she followed the girl along the row of houses. By the state of her clothes, the woman was in trade. No political colours, but the clothes weren't patched or worn. Unlike many, she went without a hat, thick blonde hair tumbling around her face and shoulders.

He fell in behind her. There was no need to hide his pursuit from the woman.

He could challenge her, find out why she was following the girl, but she'd reveal her reasons soon enough. As soon as the girl led them to wherever they were going.

He felt in his pockets for his pistols.

The woman had slowed. Kemp slowed.

They would be out on Palace Walk soon. Why was the girl leading them into Eldereham? What business did someone from the Bogs have there? She couldn't hope to hide.

The girl entered Palace Walk, and the woman quickly followed.

A bell rang out from the west.

The Palace bell. It struck time and time again. Nine. Ten. Eleven times.

Kemp's steps faltered. His captain had said she'd need everyone to be near the Palace Bridge by Half-past Eleven. The comte would be arriving and they needed eyes on the crowd.

He looked to where the girl and the woman were already disappearing ahead.

He'd have to hurry if he was to catch them.

Can't risk it. Take too long to follow them.

But what if they're…

He shook the thought away. No point in wasting time on suspicion when the captain definitely needed him at the bridge.

He turned in the opposite direction and headed back toward the Up Hibourne.

III

The Down Hibourne ditch, Palace district

The young 'Fisher flicked open his pocket watch as the Palace bell chimed. "Half an hour until the comte," he said to his group of compatriots as they made their way through the crowds back towards the Palace Bridge.

How could you know? Burston asked in his mind as he followed behind. *Not even I know, and I work at the Palace.* They were oblivious to him. They seemed oblivious to everyone it seemed, expecting the masses to part before them. *Except it's always around Half-past Eleven.* He swatted the thought away.

A passing shoulder struck him. He jabbed at the passer by's ankle to remind him to watch where he was going, and strode on. But that seemed to be the way with everyone.

Enough time had passed since he'd left the area beyond the bridge, he was sure. Even if not, he'd be safer there, away from the masses, only the people of quality to worry about. His arse and leg still ached.

Why did you help her? It had taken some time while searching for a watchman for Burston to recognise who had helped the thief. It was uncommon for Everett to come to the Palace, but Burston was sure that it was the banker who had helped the thief. *Why help that piece of bogs' shit?*

On realising it had been Everett, he had been left with two choices: report the banker to the Watch, see Everett pay his way out and turn the blame on Burston; or swallow his shame at the assault and find some other way to get reimbursement for the trouble from Everett. There would no doubt be a need to inspect the structure of Everett's bank, make sure it was not hazardous to the public's wellbeing.

The 'Fisher's were wittering on about the comte. Did they really expect some show from Vasini's leader? He'd make some speech, but it would be the same one he always made when addressing the people beyond the bridge on the first day of the Fayre.

They were nearing the Palace attendants in their white, yellow and blue livery. The 'Fishers' staff were already hurrying forward to pay the toll to reach the ice beyond.

Burston pulled in closer to the group, bowing his head, hoping he would be counted amongst their number.

There was an unheard exchange between the lead attendant and the lead valet from the 'Fishers' staff. Money was quickly exchanged, and the attendants ushered the group on.

Burston continued with them, but, as he passed an attendant, a hand was lowered before him, blocking his path.

"Monsieur Burston?" The attendant asked.

"Yes."

"I am sorry, I need your payment. It is just a formality. Shilling only. I am sure —"

"I have already been beyond the bridge today." Burston met the attendant's eyes. They were a bright blue. The attendant didn't flinch.

"The payment is for each passage. I am sure —"

"I am a man of the Palace."

"I am sure that you understand then that payment must be taken."

The attendant's eyes remained fixed on his, her hand extended for payment.

"I am a servant of the city."

The attendant still did not move her hand.

Other 'Fishers and Scarlets appeared around him, paying the other attendants for their entry. Burston's shoulders sagged and his head slumped to stare at the snow. He felt in his pocket for his purse. Given the day he was having, he could ill afford to create a scene in front of those who led the city.

His pocket lay flat. He padded himself, trying not to show his confusion.

The girl.

She'd taken it.

He had no money on him.

She —

He looked at the attendant, whose hand remained held forward insistent on coin. His jaw moved, trying to utter something, but no words were forthcoming.

The shit. The. Shit!

"Monsieur?" The attendant asked, her stern look becoming one of puzzlement.

Burston's jaw continued to work in silence. Finally, he turned and walked away, trying not to fall as a light-headedness swept over him.

Palace Walk, Eldereham district

Claire cast a look back again, trying to glimpse the man in the greatcoat. He was gone. She was sure now. She didn't know when he'd stopped following the girl, after he had slowed and forced Claire to take the lead, but he was gone now. There was no sign of the girl's rescuer either.

Maybe he hadn't been following her?

Maybe he realised I was following? Why slow down, unless he did? I could've scared him off.

But he'll have seen me.

She forced the thoughts down.

With neither man there, she could approach the girl, find out the source of the commotion and why they were interested in her.

Assuming it's not that I just can't see them.

She forced the thought away. "Excuse me," she called to the girl's back before the thoughts could return.

The girl carried on.

"'Scuse me," Claire said again, picking up speed. She reached out, but, before her hand touched the girl, the girl turned.

A blade was in the girl's hand.

Claire stepped back, her attention locked on the blade. The dull metal swiped forward.

Claire stepped back, nearly stumbling. She forced herself to look the girl in the eyes. "I'd like to buy you some food."

The girl's jaw dropped. Her face creased with confusion, fear setting in her eyes.

Claire raised her hands to show she posed no threat.

The girl's face hardened, the fear twisting her mouth into a grimace.

"I want to help you. I saw what happened. Can I buy you food?"

"Why?" The girl's voice was harsh, shrill, forcing itself out from her taught lips.

"I want to help." Claire kept her hands raised.

"Why?" The girl was almost pleading now.

"You seem like you need some," Claire said.

The girl stood unable to speak, just holding out the blade.

Claire looked around. They were close to The Lychway. They were too low in Eldereham to be near any coffee shops. The closest source of food would be the Fayre. She dipped in her pocket and pulled out two pence. "Can I get you some pig roast?"

The girl didn't react.

"My name's Claire."

The girl nodded.

Claire headed for The Lychway, hoping that by heading for the river by a different route it would stop them stumbling across the other pursuers. The girl followed.

The Down Hibourne ditch, Palace district

Burston's face was warm. He couldn't help the sense of embarrassment, of the wrongness of what he was doing. But damn that girl to Mhal, he was not going to let her thievery stop him from being at the comte's speech. His face burned at invoking the name of the old god.

He had made his way back towards the Palace and then slipped into the woodland that surrounded it, finding his way back towards the Down Hibourne, above the Palace Bridge.

He watched the attendants near the bridge, making sure their attentions were focused on the steady flow of red and blue that was now making its way to see the comte and then lowered himself carefully from the bank to the snow covered ice.

Burston straightened himself, his face still flushed. He cast look after look at the bridge, still not quite believing he'd managed to avoid detection so easily, and hurried as quickly as his unsteady feet would allow towards where the crowds were gathering in their groups of red and blue.

As he approached, the attention of the assembly turned towards the bank from which he'd strode. *Someone's seen me. They're going —*

They were looking past him to the bank proper.

Burston turned to follow their gazes. Down the bank, a small group had appeared. At least Burston thought they had. It was difficult to make them out, their bodies seemed to merge with the snow.

They're in white? Why was the whole group wearing the comte's colours?

A hush had fallen across the crowd as they continued to watch the comte approach. Seigneur Gallieni and his wife walked next to the comte.

Where's Gallieni's blues? He —

It struck him, as it seemed to strike the crowd based on the surge of whispering.

He's converted. He's showing support for the comte. But…

Burston's mind faltered, unable to quite process what the scene meant.

The comte and the Gallienis stepped slowly down the bank and onto the ice.

Someone broke away from the crowd, stepping forward to greet them.

A woman.

Renard?

The blue coat slipped from about her, tumbling to the snow, to reveal white underneath.

The murmurs grew to a full onslaught of muttering and exclamation.

But —?

Burston's mind still refused to process what he was seeing.

Renard. Gallieni. They're... They're Fishers.

So is the comte.

But... They should be wearing blue.

White...

The crowd was surging forward. Angry words were barked at Gallieni and Renard.

Burston felt his feet carry him forward, joining with the surge towards the comte's group.

His faction?

Two more, dressed in white, had stepped forward from the crowd.

The Lychway, Eldereham district

Everett looked about, unsure of what to do. He'd lost her. He was sure now. He'd lost sight of her on Palace Walk. He'd carried on until the Walk reached The Lychway, but hadn't caught sight of her again. She must have doubled back to the river.

Why had she run from him?

Everett had first encountered the girl at the Winter Fayre three years ago. He'd caught her, quite by accident, picking a Scarlet's pocket, a glimpse of her hand holding a purse after she'd bumped into the unsuspecting woman. The girl had disappeared amongst the crowd before he'd even been able to raise an alarm. He'd put it out of his mind for the rest of the day, until he'd felt someone catch his side. He'd turned to see the girl's face disappearing into the crowd and discovered he no longer had his purse. It had been pointless to report the girl, by the time he'd found a watchman she could have been lost in the streets of any of the four districts that marked the boundary of the Fayre. So he'd let her go and put her out of his mind.

That was until the Fayre the next year, when he caught sight of a pickpocket. He had been passing a young woman as he saw the hand slip into a coat pocket. On instinct, he had reached out to grab the interloping hand, but had stopped short when he had seen the thief's face — that of his own pickpocket the year before. She hadn't even looked at him, just hurried on into the crowd, the young woman oblivious to her loss.

Last year, Everett had thought to look for the girl, unsure what he'd do with her when he saw her. He'd had to visit the Fayre on three consecutive days before finding her plying her trade near a pig roast. She'd grown in the intervening year. Once barely up to his chest, she was now past his shoulders but remained thin. He had watched her for hours, carefully following her to see what she would do, trying to understand why she'd risk her life, risk being hung in Sullivan's Court Square, even if the money would put food in her belly. He had to admire her bravery and her skill.

And now he'd tried to help her, to keep her from the gallows, and she'd run.

Why? He'd scared her maybe? Maybe she didn't realise he was helping? He needed to make sure she was safe. But he couldn't if he couldn't find her.

If his intervention had been enough to scare her, perhaps she'd have given in for the day. In which case, he'd never find her today.

If not, she'd be looking to ply her trade again. Everett's feet were already carrying him back towards the Hibourne and the Fayre. Maybe he could check some of the stalls she seemed to favour.

The Down Hibourne ditch, Palace district

The comte and his contingent of white-clad supporters were surrounded by red and blue. Kemp cast a look up at the bridge. A string of Third Fusiliers looked down, many of them resting against the bridge wall, but their muskets close by, ready to shoot even a 'Fisher or Scarlet if they saw an attack heading for the comte or Gallieni.

Kemp stood the other side of the bridge, watching through the archways as the red and blue swarmed around the figures in white. He snatched a glance at the attendants, their attention was fixed on the ruckus as well. He slipped beneath an archway, keeping close to a pillar, using it to block the view of the attendants, who were drifting towards the other side of the bridge as well.

A box or stool had appeared from somewhere for the comte to stand on to raise him up a little above the heads of the crowd.

A hush came across the crowd. The voice of the comte, faint from this distance, drifted across to where Kemp stood, back against the pillar.

Others had begun to come through beneath the bridge, drawn by the crowd of blue and red. The attendants hadn't noticed or didn't care as no one attempted to stop the surge of the masses.

This was not good, more crowds meant greater risk, greater chance that someone would start a riot.

Kemp let himself be drawn along with masses.

The noise from the crowd had quietened until the comte tried to speak, at which point the masses had roared again. Burston had joined the ranks of the 'Fishers and Scarlets. No one seemed to care about his presence, their concentration fixed on the sight of the new political alliance.

"Our city can no longer —" The comte started, but his voice was drowned out by a swell in the crowd's roar.

Burston pressed forward, trying to get closer to hear what the comte had to say about the turn of events. A row of red backs blocked his way. His arm lifted on instinct, the pommel of his cane lancing towards the nearest red coat, as he pushed forward again.

"Our divisions —" The comte's voice filtered through the shouts.

"Traitors," a man screamed to Burston's left.

The red coat in front of him whirled on Burston as his cane pommel made contact.

The eyes blazed with fury. The Scarlet's mouth opened, spittle flew out as he shouted at Burston, hitting Burston on the cheek. But Burston could not hear the words.

Other Scarlets turned on him, men and women. Faces vague but familiar.

Pain lanced through his side.

His arm pulled back to clutch at the pain, acting of its own accord. The cane fell to the snow.

His head swung to find the source. A woman, in red, was pulling back from him.

Burston's legs were numb, the strength had left them.

Faces swam around him — familiar and strange. Red everywhere.

He stumbled back and fell on his arse.

Kemp was too late. He had seen the figure in red's hand lance out just as the man in black stepped forward. The knife had cut into the man in black's side.

The figure in red was already backing out of the crowd as the man in black — *Burston?* — stumbled and fell to his arse, clutching at his side. The crowd parted from him, trying to avoid him at first, not noticing what was going on, too caught up in launching insults at the comte and his supporters.

Kemp ran for the figure in red.

Someone in the crowd shouted out. The stabbed man — *He's having a bad day if it is Burston* — had been noticed.

Kemp's boots fought for grip as he moved across the snow-covered ice.

See me, his mind screamed out to the guards atop the bridge. *See him.* But no shot came.

The figure was heading for the Palace bank.

Kemp's breath plumed out in front of him, his breathing already heavy with the exertion of moving across the snow.

He came to the bank. Still no one seemed to have noticed them.

He planted his hands into the snow and levered himself up, glancing up to see the flash of red running on towards woodland.

Kemp found his feet again and hurried on, his hands dipping into his pockets to find his pistols.

Red flashed amongst the trees.

The pistols were in Kemp's hands.

He fired.

Bark splintered.

The red continued to run.

Kemp stopped, allowing him to steady his aim.

He fired.

The crack echoed amongst the woodland.

There was a thud.

The red tumbled to the ground.

IV

The Down Hibourne ditch, Palace district

Burston gripped at the pain in his side, clamping his eyes shut against the welling tears. He would not show weakness. He would impress on them how strong he was.

Hands grabbed beneath his arms and pulled him up.

On instinct, Burston flailed, trying to drive the unseen force away.

Pain exploded in his side, and he clamped his hand down on his hip again.

He found himself in a chair.

"I —" Pain cut off Burston's words. The snow around seemed brilliant, his vision turning white. Was it snowing again? Was it colder?

He tried to speak again, but a voice behind called out "We need a barber. He's bleeding."

Palais de Vasini, Palace district

The figure in red remained sprawled next to the tree. The snow to one side was turning pink.

Kemp kept a pistol levelled at the figure. He hadn't had a chance to reload, but the figure did not know that.

Ya dead?

Kemp stepped forward. Plumes of white billowed from his mouth as he recovered from the exertion of his pursuit.

The figure remained prone.

Kemp stepped forward again.

Still no movement.

Ya're dead. Shit.

He could see the shot hole in the left shoulder.

Shot shouldn't have killed him.

And as if to confirm the thought, the body groaned.

Kemp fell to his knees next to the body, placing the still warm gun barrel against the figure's neck.

Closer now, he could see the figure's neck and legs were slender compared to the upper body. The red coat was too big for the rest of the body. A woman.

With his free hand he pulled at the collar of the coat, revealing a brown coat beneath. *Gonna get rid of the red and hide in brown?*

"Why'd you stab him?"

The woman groaned again.

"He wasn't in blue."

The woman was unresponsive.

It was pointless talking with her here.

Kemp rose to his feet, grabbing the woman's closest hand as he did. He pulled her arm, dragging her semi-conscious body up so he could sling her over his shoulder.

The Up Hibourne ditch, Palace district

Hat's belly strained as she licked the grease from her fingers. She felt warm, properly warm, stood by the fire of the pig roast. She let a belch escape as the bacon, bread and mulled wine settled in her.

The woman — Claire — raised an eyebrow at the sound, licking her own fingers clean.

"What?" Hat asked, expecting the woman to come back at her and tell her off for her bad manners, like the Barker would, or Cas.

"Are you ready to talk?"

Hat stood in silence, unsure how to respond.

"Will you tell me your name?"

Hat remained silent, searching for something in Claire's face that might tell Hat she could trust the woman.

"It's just your name."

"Hat," Hat said, still unsure whether to trust Claire.

"Hello, Hat," Claire said, offering her hand.

Hat ignored it.

"Why were there people after you?" Claire asked.

"Ya know why."

"If I did, I wouldn't ask."

"Ya expect me to say it 'ere? Too many ears."

The woman seemed to sag, a plume of white escaping her nose as she snorted a sigh. "You stole. But why did the man help you?"

Hat's eyes darted about, expecting to see a watchman snatch her on hearing what the woman claimed. She spoke through gritted teeth. "It's ta eat." *And pay the Barker.*

"I know."

"Then why ask?" Hat made to walk away, but Claire moved to block her.

"Why did the man help you?"

"I don' know," Hat replied, hanging her head. Her face was warm. She hoped it was the mulled wine and food, but she knew it was embarrassment. Why did she feel embarrassed for not knowing why some lunatic had helped her? She'd been lucky. But why had he helped? Why bother with her? "I don' know," she said again.

"Did you recognise him?"

Hat shook her head.

"Do you want to find out why?"

What? "Get myself in trouble?"

"Why —?"

"I count my luck and don' push it. If he wanted to help me, so be it. I'm not gonna look for trouble."

Hat shoved her hand out to push past Claire.

Claire reached out to stop her, but Hat pushed on, bursting into a run to get away from the woman.

Leave me. Got work to do. Can't be bothering with why people do stupid things.

She didn't look back as the woman called after her.

The Down Hibourne ditch, Palace district

Susan saw him first. She was holding Isaac's hand, keeping him from falling as they skeeted close to the bank. The crease in her brow and the glance to Anna at the side of the skeeting area said it all. His family knew he had disappeared. It wasn't surprising given the amount of time he had been away. Everett hoped that a simple apology, that he'd decided to walk off to look around the Fayre while they had their fun, would be enough to allay their fears.

Isaac looked up from where he was concentrating on moving his feet. As soon as he saw his father, his feet scrambled against the ice to try to propel him towards Everett, but he just slipped and slid, forcing

Susan to grab him with her other hand to hold him upright, nearly causing her to lose her balance.

Everett, wanting to help his son avoid a bruised backside, hurried forward on the snow until he was at the edge of the clear ice.

Susan was guiding Isaac carefully around the edge of the cleared area, Isaac's feet stumbling as he tried to walk rather than skeete.

"Where have you been?" Anna's voice was more chilling than the air.

Everett turned to face his wife.

"I-I'm sorry." He lowered his gaze. "I wanted to see the rest of the Fayre."

"You could have told one of us." She had moved to within an arms length of him. Someone bustled past, behind Everett, bumping him towards Anna.

"I didn't want to interrupt your fun."

"They're looking for you." Her voice was still chill.

"I'm sorry."

"Just a word. To one of us."

"I wasn't gone long."

"Long enough." She shook her head. Her voice became hushed. "You may not wear colours, but there's enough who would be happy to misbelieve you prefer red or blue. And things..." Her voice drifted, her face wincing as though she were in pain.

"What's happened?"

"I didn't see it. But I've heard them talking."

"Who?"

"The comte has allies."

"He's —"

"They wear his colours."

"How?"

"You know everything I know." She stared at him, her brow creasing. She stepped forward her hand going for his arm. "Tim—"

He was already walking away.

Her hand clamped around his wrist. "Timothy. What are you going to do that will change anything?"

"I need to know."

"For what reason?"

"People will be nervous —"

"The bank is closed. It's the first day of the Fayre. And you have a family."

"I-I have customers too."

"Who are enjoying the snow."

Isaac was close now. He'd be with them in a few moments.

Anna was right, of course. But he had to know.

He tried not to look at her or Isaac as he walked away.

"Send Richard," Anna called after him.

With every step, warmth flooded to Everett's face. He hung his head, trying not to hear his wife. *They need to say what they stand for now. They can't just create something. People need to know. They have to have some certainty over what the comte will do. Where he will lead the city.*

The Up Hibourne ditch, Palace district

Hat's feet moved slowly, almost sliding rather than walking. She still felt fat from the food. Her eyes drifted from one person to the next, her mind not really recognising what she saw. There was part of her that wanted to leave, to go back to the house. But the Barker would be there, and she couldn't stand the way his voice cut through her head when he shouted for his money.

Others from the house would be here by now. She could find them, maybe join up and hit some groups. Maybe Kitty would want to.

But the strangeness of the day, the way that man had tripped her target. Tried to save her. Did save her.

And the woman.

Claire.

Why'd they want to help me?

She winced against the thought, shaking it from her head. *Don't think like that. Don't… It'll lead to badness. They'll sploit ya and…*

She forced the thoughts from her mind, focusing on the crowd around her.

A group of red bustled through the crowd, ignoring those around them, hurrying for some unseen place.

Hat watched them move, falling in behind them.

They were too tightly packed, barely a gap between their shoulders. They murmured to each other as they nearly ran through the Fayre. Several others followed in their wake. No doubt their servants.

Hat turned from them, searching out another target.

The Down Hibourne ditch, Palace district

Claire rolled her shoulders, stretching out her arms to her sides. She felt uncomfortable in her body. The way Hat had run had thrown her. She'd tried to think her way through things as she searched for the girl, but her mind was as unsettled as her body.

Claire tried to calm her mind, trying to focus on a moment of stillness around her as Sarah — her and Jacob's elder — had taught. But there was too much movement, too much agitation, in the crowd.

There was a glimpse of thin movement ahead.

That her?

Claire tried to dart between two people before the movement disappeared, but the gap was closed and, when it opened again, whoever it had been was lost amongst the surge.

Claire glanced about.

A hand shoved her from behind.

She whirled, nearly slipping on the ice, to find a thickset older man ready to shove her forward again, his warty face twisted into a scowl.

"Move," the man said.

"Go around," Claire said back, glancing around for sight of the girl.

The man shoved her shoulder. "Can't go round. Look at it."

Claire went to say something back, but stopped herself when she realised the oddity in the flow of people. Everyone was heading in the same direction. Vendors were abandoning their stalls.

Everyone was surging upriver.

"What's happened?" Claire asked, realising now that something had to be wrong to cause this. "Why are they evacuating?"

People behind the thickset man were shouting now, demanding that they both move.

The man's face creased with confusion. "What shit ya talking? 'Vacuating? Ain't ya heard the 'nouncement."

"What?"

"Move," the man shoved past.

Claire, unable to stand against the surge, turned quickly, so as not to be shoved down, and followed the flow of people.

What's going on?

What's happening?

There was a crack from ahead, echoing out above the murmur and shouts of the crowd.

Gunfire?
Or the ice?
Is the ice cracking?

They had not fired on the crowd. Everett was sure of that.
They wouldn't be so stupid.
They'd risk a riot.

The crowd pressed in around him as it continued to surge up the Down Hibourne. Whatever had happened had not deterred the crowd.

The announcement. The risk of riots.
They'll lose stability.
People will get nervous.
They get nervous at a fly in their soup.
They'll —

There was another crack and the chatter of the crowd became a roar.

This is it.
Here we go.

Everett's eyes closed, blocking out the sight of the violence to come.

But it didn't.

He wasn't struck.

Everett opened his eyes, blinking with surprise at the lack of a blow.

I must have misheard.
I —

The crowd had come to a stop.

"What's happening up there?" He asked the woman, swaddled in a greatcoat, in front.

She turned and shrugged.

"Ask," Everett said, the immediate panic letting go of his innards, allowing him to switch to the 'Gentleman of Authority' role he played at the bank.

The woman turned and asked the thin man in front. The thin man told her he didn't know. As the woman turned to relay the message, Everett told the thin man to ask the light-haired man in front of him.

With a few more instructions, Everett had sent a ripple of enquiries through the crowd.

Everett checked his watch. Within four minutes people were turning to those behind. The ripple had rebounded and was returning to him.

Three people turned towards the woman in the greatcoat, bombarding her with chatter.

"Someone was shot —"

"They're dead —"

"Someone went for the comte —"

"— Red and blues were fighting —"

"— Scarlet ran off —"

"— Stabbed—"

Everett had heard enough. *I'm not going to get any sense from them.*

As the perplexed woman in the greatcoat turned to relay the information to him, Everett headed sideways. He could see people were already lining the Palace banks. They were in green.

The Watch. At least it was the Watch and not the Regiment.

They'd let him through, and he could find someone who could provide some useful information.

Maybe Marcus is there. He'll get some sense into them.

Palais de Vasini, Palace district

As his senses came back to him, there was the chiming of a great bell.

The Palace bell?
Is it noon already?

Burston glanced about the small room in which he'd been left. There'd been a lot of fuss around him. Someone had torn his clothes away and another had pulled a length of catgut from a leather bag and stitched his side. It had been a blur if he was honest with himself, the throbbing heat in his side absorbing his attention. His side was still red hot. Once the stitching had been completed, they'd bound him with bandages and abandoned him.

They had found a chair for him from somewhere, he remembered. Unceremoniously, he'd been hoisted on to it and then carried up the Palace bank and off towards the Palace itself. He'd been aware of someone putting pressure on his side, pressing against the wound. His vision, though, had remained a blur of white and the voices had been distant. It had taken all of his concentration to maintain his balance on the chair.

Am I supposed to find my own person to tend to me now? Burston thought as no one appeared. He wasn't quite sure where he was in the Palace. He thought that he was on the ground floor — he had no memory of them lifting him up the stairs, only the entrance steps. They'd taken a right, he thought, so he was in the servants' wing where all of the staff who maintained the Palace worked. He realised he'd never been in this part of the Palace.

His backside was becoming uncomfortable on the chair, another discomfort along with his throbbing side. He tried to raise himself, but his body refused.

Burston looked about for his cane, but after awhile realised that it had likely been left down on the river.

Some bogs' shit has probably taken it. Like my coin.

Damn this day.

Damn it to —

The door opened, and a woman in white entered.

"Monsieur Burston?" The woman asked.

She looked and sounded like Emma Renard.

"Oui. Madame…?" Burston asked, hoping she would offer her name. This woman was wearing white rather than Renard's blue.

The woman's mouth twinged with amusement. "I see that you are still shocked by events."

If this were Renard, why would she be here to see him?

"I am on the mend," Burston said, straightening himself in the chair to try to present a strong front.

"I am glad that the barber-surgeon I provided has turned around your circumstances."

"The barber was yours? Then I owe you my thanks…Madame…?" Burston tried the question again.

The woman's mouth broadened into a proper smile. "If it were different circumstances, I would feel slighted by your memory."

"My apologies. Madame…?"

"Renard."

It was. It was Renard. But she was in white.

The comte. The announcement.

His face flushed. He could not make eye contact with her. *Foolish, stupid mind.*

"Do not feel bad, Monsieur Burston." She walked towards him.

Why are you here?

"It seems my aides have not provided me with a chair. I will need to speak with them."

Burston looked about and realised he did occupy the only seat. He shoved a hand onto the seat and tried to lever himself up.

"Please, no, monsieur," Renard raised a hand to stop him. "You are injured."

"But you —"

"No, monsieur. Better that you sit."

Burston scrutinised her, unsure whether she truly meant the gesture or if he should continue to vacate the chair. The throbbing in his side made the decision, and he collapsed back into the seat.

"I have a few questions for you."

I'm of use to her. She needs me. "I would be honoured to help you, madame."

"You were attacked."

"Yes," Burston said before realising it wasn't a question.

"Did you recognise your attacker?"

"No. It was…was too quick."

"Did you see their colours?"

"They were red."

"Are you sure?"

No. No. "Yes." He wouldn't let his mind give in to indecision.

Renard thought on his response for a moment. "Have you had issues with Scarlets?"

"My duty is to those who pay for this city," Burston said, hoping his words were suitable for Renard's politics.

Her face remained stoic. "Have you heard anything?"

"In…in what way?"

"Rumours. Speculation."

"There is much discussed at the Palace."

"About me?"

"Not of recent times. Not of any substance." *What is she after?*

"May I ask a question?"

Renard gave a nod of permission.

"Your colours have changed."

"That is a statement of fact, I believe."

"You share the comte's colours."

"We share colours."

"Then you have left the blue?"

Renard's eyes narrowed.

I've stepped too far.

Renard's eyes relaxed. "Neither blue, nor indeed red, flatter the complexion." Renard thought for a moment. "Thank you." She thought a moment more. "I hope your wounds heal quickly."

"Thank you for your assistance."

Renard gave a distracted smile, turned and exited.

Burston waited. *Is that it? Do I go? Is someone coming to tend to me some more?*

Horses snorted in the stalls as Kemp sat on an upturned bucket waiting for Stone, one of the regimental barber's, to finish with the woman. Stone was taking her time and was still muttering about having to perform surgery in a stable.

Kemp had rushed the body of the attacker to the Palace stables, wanting to hide her before the Watch or the Inspectorate arrived. It had been the standing orders since the events last December after the death of Vittoria Emerson and Robert Hume: if an attack involving a 'Fisher or Scarlet was witnessed, take control of the situation before the Inspectorate could. He did not know his superiors' reasoning, but suspected the orders had come down from the Palace, which meant that the comte didn't want the Inspectorate involved.

"Finished," Stone said, emerging from the stall, wiping her hands down with a cloth.

"Thank ya," Kemp said, knocking the bucket over as he rose. "Let the captain know."

Stone nodded and collected her bag of tools from the stall.

As Stone departed, Kemp looked down at his captive sprawled out on the stall floor.

Wavy red hair cascaded about her pallid round face. Her eyes were half-closed, but Kemp suspected that she was feigning semi-consciousness to dissuade him from talking to her. Stone had removed the captive's coats to deal with her wounds. The red coat was now draped over her, covering much of her body. The brown coat was nowhere to be seen; Kemp assumed it was beneath her.

"Are ya from Manis?" Kemp asked. It was a possibility with the red hair.

"Vasini, born and bred," the woman mumbled.

"But ya got their blood?"

The woman's eyes opened fully then narrowed, scrutinising Kemp. She didn't respond.

"Red's not ya colour," Kemp said, kicking at her coat.

The woman continued to scrutinise him for a moment, then looked away.

Kemp sighed, exaggerating the gesture by putting his hands on his hips. "Ya just gonna get cold. See, I have ya prisoner. I can hold ya like this till ya talk. Don't talk, ya lie there and ya freeze."

The woman turned her attention back to him. "Ya'll freeze with me."

Not bloody likely. Captain will show soon, and then ya'll get dragged off. Probably up river, and they'll stick ya in gaol, with no one around, ta rot.

"Ya Ranter?"

"Just 'cause I'm not a Scarlet?"

"Who else is there 'part from Scarlets, 'Fishers and Ranters?"

"Ask the comte."

The woman looked away again.

Kemp crouched down at the woman's feet. He caught her eye and stared at her, trying to make some sense of what happened. "Ya no 'Fisher, Scarlet or Ranter. Ya went for some man in a crowd that didn't have colours. So why'd ya do it?"

"I didn't."

"Ya denying ya stabbed a man?"

"Why should I admit it?"

She had a point. Why should she admit her crime? She'd be found guilty and likely hang, if she was lucky. If she was unlucky, she'd disappear to be some nameless prisoner up in the Rivergate gaol. It didn't matter what she said. "Who did it then?"

"Don't know what ya're talking about."

The conversation was boring Kemp. The captain would be here soon and then his duty would be done. He stood up, shaking his legs to wake them up, then started to pace the area just outside the stall.

"Let's assume ya did it," Kemp said. "Let's assume that ya're not a Scarlet. So you want a Scarlet to take the blame. Which suggests ya're a 'Fisher or a Ranter."

The woman remained silent.

"Likely reason ya'd want to lay blame at the Scarlets for the attack. 'Cept Ranters would likely want them to know it was one of them. No point in making an attack 'gainst the 'stablishment if they think it was someone from the 'stablishment that did it. So that leaves it as a 'Fisher. But ya don't look like 'Fisher. So that means ya were paid."

The woman remained silent.

"Silence isn't gonna save ya."

The woman remained silent.

Could make her talk.

Kemp looked at her, thinking about how to go about extracting information from her then gave up. He should wait for the captain. He wouldn't want to break her if the captain had other plans for her.

Kemp paced the stables as he waited.

V

The Down Hibourne ditch, Palace district

Now that Claire was reaching the front, the crowd was dispersing. The Watch had arrived and, with crossbows in hand, were guiding people back to the right side of the bridge. Only those dressed in red or blue were allowed to remain.

Yet oddly, it seemed, it was the red and the blue who were most likely to cause the police issues. They had formed into loose groups, standing near the banks — red to the right, blue to the left. As the members of each group stood talking with each other, some would glance over to their political rivals. Hands were held inside coats, or in padded pockets.

Weapons, Claire realised. It had been Jacob who had spent much of his time keeping an eye on the people of quality, leaving Claire to watch the traders from the other city-states, but she had some knowledge of how the animosity between the Scarlets and 'Fishers manifested itself. You could not escape it in Vasini.

Two watchmen were turning a young couple away, the watchmen's crossbows pointed at the floor to appear less threatening. As the couple turned, Claire stepped into their path and then fell in beside them.

"What happened?" She asked, trying to sound only half-interested so as not to raise suspicions with her enthusiasm for information.

"Not much," one of the men said. The two men tried to move away, but Claire carried on with them.

"Who got shot?"

"Huh?" The man who had spoken, turned to look at her, biting at his lip with annoyance.

"There were gunshots."

"Someone got stabbed. And a Scarlet ran off."

"But the gun shot?" Claire asked.

The man held out his gloved hand.

His companion smiled and shook his head, amused by his partner.

Does everything have to cost money? Claire thought as she fished out her coin pouch and handed over a penny.

The talking man kept his hand held out.

Claire placed another penny in it.

The hand remained.

Claire dropped a ha'penny in and then stared at the man, making sure he understood she wouldn't be parted with any more coins.

"The 'Fishers started at the Scarlets as soon as they saw someone in red running away. Looked like there was going to be violence. A Scarlet went for a 'Fisher, but one of his friends fired a pistol into the air. The look on the Scarlet's face was funny, thought he'd shit himself, and the other Scarlets were about to go for the 'Fisher. 'Cept another gun goes off in the air, and everyone then turns to this watchman who'd appeared. Don't know why he'd have a pistol. A couple of reds and a couple blues then started at the watchman, shouting at him. Then all the watchmen turn up and spoil the fun."

He grinned at his companion.

"Is that all?" Claire asked.

"All ya're going to get," the man said before he walked off arm in arm with his companion.

The two men walked faster, diverting from their path to get away from Claire.

Claire came to a stop, thinking on what she'd been told. *The Scarlets and Fishers have probably taken their fights into the alleys, away from the eyes of the Watch.* She wouldn't be too surprised if come the morning the newssheets were reporting on more attacks than just the one that had happened here.

"I'd have told ya that for less," a woman's voice said from beside her.

Claire sagged. She could have done without the interjection.

"For that amount I'd have told ya more," the woman's voice said.

Claire glanced at the woman. She was swaddled in layers of clothes. Her wrinkled face was bony and sharp. Grey hair peaked out from beneath her cap.

"How do I know you know anything?" Claire asked, hoping the challenge might prompt the woman to reveal something free of charge.

The woman's eyes twinkled with amusement, then her face twisted into a smile. "It's a risk ya'll have to take."

Claire gave it a moment's thought, then turned and walked away. She had no time for bluffers and con people.

Palais de Vasini, Palace district

It had taken nearly an hour for Everett to reach the Palace. The Palace Watch who had lined the Palace bank of the Hibourne had proven reluctant to let him past. He'd eventually convinced them to seek out someone at the Palace to confirm his credentials. The wait for the watchman's return had left him dwelling on the thought that he'd abandoned Anna and his family. He should have been with them, but he needed to make some sense of events before they got out of hand.

The Palace was abandoned, the halls near silent, when Everett managed to convince the regimental guard to let him through the front door. No doubt the majority of the staff were at the Fayre.

Where to try first? Everett thought as he stood at the bottom of the grand staircase in the entrance hall. He could go straight to the comte, but it could be seen as presumptive of him to demand an audience. And, no doubt, there were 'Fishers and Scarlets already demanding to speak to him over the announcement. There was Marcus, but would he even be here? The hearings to confirm him as the new commandant were still taking place. He was yet to take his place in the commandant's office, and was still working at the Palace district police offices. Where would the seigneurs and médiateurs be? With the comte? In talks with their allies over the happenings with the comte and the attacks? The staff of the Baronnie du Trésor were likely down at the Fayre.

Have I wasted the walk? Everett asked himself, the sense that he should be back with Anna strengthening.

If I'm here, though, I can try something.

He started up the stairs, planning his journey so as not to waste the effort required for the ascent. He'd already had to walk so far from the banks of the Hibourne.

Two floors up to the Baronnie de Justice.

The Comte on the fifth.
Then the Baronnie du Trésor in the attic.

Why the Treasury had to be in the roof of the Palace, Everett had no idea. He needed to have Marcus or pay someone to invent a device that would make travelling up the flights of stairs easier on him.

Everett started up the stairs, keeping a steady pace, knowing not to let himself give in to his eagerness lest he exhaust himself halfway to his goal.

The first staircase out of the way, he turned to follow the landing round to the next staircase.

Voices came from above. A discussion between two women.

"It is a simple matter," one woman said. A recognisable voice, but the name slipped out of Everett's grasp, tormenting him. "We are seeking to move beyond the two factions that have split our city."

"By creating a third?" The other woman asked. This woman's voice was not recognisable and lacked the refined tone of the first.

"By putting aside the barriers that two colours have created between the city's leadership," the first woman said.

Everett found his feet slowing. It would be rude for him to interrupt.

"We are neither blue nor red," the first woman continued. "We are only interested in the betterment of the city. Not the principle of opposition that exists between the Scarlets and 'Fishers." The name of the woman came to him. It was Renard's daughter, Emma.

"Many will see this as just a way of distancing yourselves from the events with the *Visages Pâle*."

Everett was at the bottom of the next staircase. Should he go up and risk interrupting the discussion, or would it be more improper to listen to the conversation between the two women without making his presence known?

"It is our way of distancing ourselves from all of the poor politics of the city."

"Thank you," the unrecognised woman said. "I think I have enough."

"It will be in tomorrow's issue?" Emma Renard asked as Everett started up the stairs.

"I doubt there will be anything more news worthy that happens today," the second woman said.

Renard gave out a light laugh. "Then I look forward to reading *The Herald* over luncheon."

"Thank you for your time, Madame Renard."

There was the sound of a moving chair as Everett crested the stairs and turned onto the landing.

Set in a small alcove, Renard placed a fine porcelain cup on the table in front of her and rose from the high-backed chair. A shorter woman — blonde hair, pulled neatly into a ponytail, tied with a blue ribbon — had already risen and was extending a gloved hand to Renard. They shook hands as Renard noted his presence with a smile.

She was wearing white. She was wearing the comte's colours. Renard was one of these new supporters of the comte. *I wonder what her father thinks?*

The shorter woman — a reporter from *The Herald* it seemed — turned to see at whom Renard was glancing. "Monsieur Everett?" The woman asked. She stepped from the alcove, offering her hand. "Jacqueline Swinton of *The Herald*."

Everett ignored the offered hand. He had little time or interest in speaking with someone from the newssheets.

"Would you happen to have any thoughts on the comte's — and Madame Renard's —" She glanced back at Renard with a smile that was making too much effort to be charmingly polite. "— Announcement?"

"No," Everett said, holding his hands behind his back. It was better that he kept his response short lest he give free rein to his vitriol towards the newssheets and their parasitic staff.

Swinton recoiled at his terseness. She looked back to Renard then excused herself with a slight bow of the head towards Renard then Everett. She departed down the stairs.

"Monsieur Everett," Renard said once Swinton had gone. "Would you join me?"

What game are you playing?

Everett took the offered seat, as Renard retook her own seat and poured herself some more tea from a pot. "Do you wish for some refreshment? I'm sure someone will come if we call?"

Has your allegiance with the comte allowed you free rein of the Palace?
"No, thank you."

"I'll be bold and assume that you are here concerning six people in white."

He wanted to shout at her, demand that she tell him what she was thinking, what they were thinking, creating even more political upheaval. "I hear someone was attacked?"

Renard's face dropped, momentarily puzzled, before taking a suitably sombre tone. "Unfortunate."

"Do you know whom?"

"A man from the Palace."

"One with connections?"

"I'm sure he would hope, but no."

"So not a response to your new colours?"

"No…Do they suit me?"

"I am not one for fashion. Maybe you should talk to my wife or my children."

The comment brought a smile to Renard's mouth, but her eyes remained analytical. "Maybe next time I am at the bank."

"I am glad that you are still a customer."

Renard's mouth twinged towards a smile again, but she didn't respond.

You're playing with me.

"I would like to know what you think of my new dress?"

"White has a way of revealing things, don't you find? Stains and the like. You will need to be careful that you do not spill anything." Everett felt tired, maintaining the innuendo of the conversation was exhausting.

"It would be useful if people were more careful not to spill things," Renard said, sipping at her tea.

"That is true." Everett watched Renard as she returned her teacup to the table, trying to determine how bold he could be. "Why change?"

"The seasons change. And fashions with them."

"You are just following trends?" Everett felt the bile rising in him, the bitterness in his mouth.

"Trying to set them."

"Does the city want to change?"

"I hope so."

He didn't want to play this game anymore. "The markets —"

The smile came to Renard's mouth again. She tilted her head as though she were questioning him.

"— The markets like the reassurance of knowing what will happen tomorrow. They prefer their trends set."

"The markets do not serve the city," Renard said.

How can you be so flippant? The markets are the city. How the money flows shapes the city. It shapes all of us.

Renard sat back in her chair. "You know white may very well suit you."

"Do you know the history of bankers wearing black?"

Renard looked momentarily stunned, not able to cope with the direct question. She gave the slightest shake of her head before regaining her poise.

"The fashion has always been that the upper classes wear strong colours, a sign of their wealth and prestige. The lower classes, the classes of the servants and the tradespeople, have worn more muted colours.

"Before the Fall, the bankers, as the holders of wealth, were licensed to wear strong colours. Many would wear as many colours as they could to show the strength of their wealth. I hate to think of the garish concoctions they would have worn.

"Many thought that upon the restoration and founding of Vasini, the bankers would continue to wear colours. And some did. Some in our fellow city-states still do. My family did not. We have always recognised that we are servants. Servants to the system of money and, through that, the city. Money defines the city. It creates its character. Where the money rests, and with whom, sets the tone, and our approach to it defines our morality.

"We are servants to that, and so we mark ourselves as servants with the most muted of colours to mark our commitment to that ideal."

He rose from his chair. He was going to get little sense from Renard.

Renard looked at him, her mouth taught, chastened it seemed.

As he walked from the alcove, Renard spoke with a weak voice: "We are in agreement."

He ignored her. He should get back to Anna and his family.

The Sini River

Hat's stomach was already beginning to feel empty again. The taste of the bacon had faded, and the warmth in her face from the mulled wine was gone. Kitty had found her out on the Sini as she watched the ebb and flow of the crowds between the Up and Down Hibournes and the Sini River. New stalls were being set up and others were being collapsed and moved in a battle to get the best spot to attract customers.

Since leaving the woman — Claire — Hat had lost interest in business. She'd feel Mabe's hand for it, for not bringing back enough for the Barker, but that was all too likely whatever she did.

Kitty kicked at Hat's feet. "We can't just sit here," Kitty said as she jabbed Hat in the side with her elbow.

Hat jabbed back. "Why not?"

"We'll freeze our arses off. Or the coppers will come decide we're menacing the passers by." She jabbed Hat's ribs again. "'Sides, it's boring."

"Well fuck off and do ya own thing then," Hat replied, returning the jab, harder. She didn't want to fight, normally she'd be up for doing something. It was just —

Kitty jabbed again, a smile on her face, apparently oblivious to Hat's frustrations. It infuriated Hat more. "Come on, we should do something. Ya hungry?"

"The Barker'll want the money."

"We'll get some more."

Hat shrugged, thinking of Claire. *Why'd she buy the food? What she really want? And the man...why'd —?*

Kitty grabbed her wrist, trying to pull Hat to her feet.

Hat let her for a moment, then pulled her hand back, yanking Kitty towards her.

"Come on." Kitty's face was scrunched up with anger.

"Ya go," Hat said. She wanted to know. None of today made sense, and she wasn't going to be able to do nothing until it did.

Kitty gave an angry yank at Hat's wrist again, but when Hat refused, she let go and stomped off through the snow that had been compacted down by the constant traffic of people.

Hat rose from where she sat, brushing snow from her backside, careful not to slip as she found her feet.

Ready, she started off towards the Down Hibourne. *Likely she's gone anyway*, Hat told herself as she headed into the crowds. *Probably just find the target who fell on his arse.*

Palais de Vasini, Palace district

Kemp didn't salute as the captain approached. Neither were in uniform, so standing orders said they shouldn't so as not to reveal they were military. Bell had nearly six inches on Kemp, her broad body though was hidden beneath loose fitting clothes, likely chosen to hide her size.

"What've you got for me?" Bell asked, waiting until she was close enough to keep her voice low.

"One who did the stabbing down on the Hibourne."

"Talking?"

Kemp shook his head.

"Sure it's the one?"

"Certain."

"Stone said you shot her?"

Kemp nodded. "Do we tell the Inspectorate?"

Bell shook her head. "I'll take it from here."

She's goin' up river, Kemp thought as he watched Bell head for the stables. "Who was stabbed?"

"A man from the Palace," Bell called back. "Burston, I think."

I wish she'd talked.

"Thank you," Bell said, not using his rank as they were out of uniform.

Would've liked to have known what she was doing stabbing someone in public like that.

Bell had disappeared through the stable door, already talking to the captive.

Kemp couldn't shake the feeling of needing to know some reason why the attack had happened. A need to make some sense of why he'd been forced into shooting the captive.

The Up Hibourne ditch, Palace district

It had been over an hour since the shots were fired, and it already seemed that the crowds on the Hibourne below the bridge to the isle of the Palace Regiment had forgotten the incident. Whether those past the bridge had put it out of their minds was yet to be seen. *It's the way of the Fayre though,* Claire mused. *An entertainment to keep us distracted.*

The thought brought a twinge of a smile. *Sounding like a Ranter.*

She had headed back to where she had been waiting for Jacob. There had been no sign of him, so, after waiting half an hour, she had started wandering the stalls. She'd had a vague thought she might see the girl again. The thought had gradually grown until she realised she was making a concerted effort to find Hat.

I shouldn't let her get in my mind like this, Claire thought as she found herself where she'd last seen Hat. She started through the crowd, trying to retrace the events with Hat.

What am I going to do with her when I find her?

She's wilful.

But she's not in a position to make use of the Path.

A contact though.

Someone on the streets, watching things.

Claire glanced about, trying to work out where Hat would have gone.

The bank opposite was the island with the fortified walls of the regimental barracks.

Although stalls lined the river along the bank, no one had taken a place on the bank itself.

So she'd have either headed up or down the river. Upwards the crowds were more compacted.

Down she went.

Claire joined a flow of fayre goers heading downstream, looking about, hoping to catch sight of some clue of where Hat would be.

She'd eaten, so she wouldn't be after food.

She was soon on the Sini.

Claire stepped out of the flow of people, joining a crowd around a makeshift open-air tavern that spread out following the bank of the regimental island.

There had to be thousands of people now swarming amongst the stalls on the Sini. Their constant chatter, the sound of music and cheers drowned out any sense in the words being spoken.

Where would she go from here?

…

Claire remained watching the swarm, hoping that she might catch a glimpse of Hat amongst the crowd. She knew, though, she was on a fool's errand — she could barely make out the faces of those closest to her, let alone those of a specific girl who may or may not have been somewhere amongst the masses.

Palais de Vasini, Palace district

Kemp had snuck into the off-duty room at the Palace and put on the uniform he'd left there earlier. It had used up time, but it was better than trying to convince the Palace staff he was a member of the Regiment despite what he was wearing.

It had taken some searching just to find someone to talk to in the Palace. They had informed Kemp that Burston was likely down on the river with most of the other Palace staff. It had taken even longer to find a second person who'd happened to see Burston after the attack. This person had revealed that Burston had been treated in the servants' wing.

Kemp hadn't found Burston when he searched the servants' wing, so he'd been forced to search the building. He'd finally found the bureaucrat sitting in a small office in the Baronnie des Bâtiments Publics et des Routes.

The man looked glum and in discomfort, his round, fleshy face contorting with little exclamations of pain as he clutched at his side. He seemed to be attempting to write something, a pen grasped in one hand hovering over a sheaf of paper. He was a portly man, his clothes tattered and bloody from the stabbing. His desk, which had simple carvings but was otherwise an unadorned affair, seemed too small for his proportions.

Kemp wasn't sure what the best way to approach such a man was, so fell back on what felt natural. "Ya survived then?" He said, attempting a light-hearted tone.

Burston looked up in shock, his mouth flapping open and closed as it searched for a response. "Yes," he finally said. "How dare you," he added.

"Ya don't want to know?" Kemp asked.

"What?" Burston looked genuinely surprised by the question.

"They got ya stabber."

"Where?" Burston asked.

Kemp just smiled back.

"Tell me."

Kemp just kept on smiling, trying to get Burston onto his back foot.

"Who do you think you are, thinking you can keep this information from me, sergeant?"

"The thing is they weren't your attacker."

"What?" Burston's jowls were wobbling with fury, his face reddening.

"Who were they going for?"

"I was the one who was stabbed."

"They had bad aim...Who was it really?"

"I was the one who was stabbed!" Burston staggered to his feet, planting his fists onto the small desk to steady himself. "I was the one stabbed, sergeant."

He just wants to feel important enough to get stabbed, Kemp realised. *Fucking witless.* "Who was near ya?"

"Where is my assailant?"

"Tell me who was near ya?"

"Why are you holding this information from me? Should I get the Watch? Should I get Marcus Fox to wring it from you? Have you heard of his alchemical abilities? I'm sure he has some trick up his sleeve to make you talk."

Truly witless. "'Cept this is regimental business. So play nice and tell me what ya know."

Burston glared at him, trying to get Kemp to speak by force of eye contact alone.

Kemp wiped at his mouth and stretched his lips out, breaking the skin where it had chapped in the cold weather. He cast a disinterested look back.

Burston's face fell as it set in that he was going to get nowhere with Kemp. "I shall speak with your captain."

"I'm sure ya will…Now what did ya see?"

Burston slumped back into his chair, forcing it backwards slightly with a screech on the wooden floor. The bureaucrat gave a wince of discomfort. "I don't —" He stopped himself, thought on his words for a moment and started again. "I only saw reds."

"What faces?"

"She…?" Burston said it as though he wanted Kemp to confirm what he was remembering was true. "It was a woman who attacked me, I think."

Burston nodded. "Did you recognise her?"

"No."

"What do you remember of her?"

"I…" Burston sat, wide-eyed and shaking his head.

He's useless as a witness. "Who was with her?"

"I…" Burston continued to shake his head.

"I just need one name."

Burston's head was still, his eyes screwed shut. He looked more like he was trying to take a shit than remember. "Canner...Theresa Canner."

Least it's something. Kemp turned, heading out of the office.

"May...May I come with you?" Burston asked.

Kemp ignored him, hoping that Burston didn't see this as consent.

The Down Hibourne ditch, Palace district

Everett had been looking forward to today, but it had soured so soon. After his exchange with Renard, he had hoped to return to his family quickly. But the trudge through the snow, navigating past the regimental guard and the Watch, then through the crowds, had taken nearly an hour and left him exhausted. His stomach was now rumbling, demanding food for his body's effort. No doubt his younger children would be harassing Anna and Susan for food as well.

Everett took a moment to catch his breath. At least the snow on the river had been trampled down into a thin carpet, so he didn't have to wade through it like he had between the Palace and the river.

I just need to find them now.

I shouldn't have been so direct with Renard. He'd had the same thought throughout his journey back. The guilt sat heavy in his chest. She was a customer, and it was of benefit to neither of them for him to be so expressive in his thoughts.

Everett had reached where his family had been skeeting. But there was no sign of Anna and his children amongst the groups of people slipping, sliding, wobbling and, often, falling across the ice.

Have they gone? The weight of guilt changed to a pang of anxiety at the thought that his family, frustrated with his continual disappearances, had abandoned him.

His stomach rumbled again, forcing a little belch from his mouth. It prompted the thought again that maybe they had gone to find food. He looked for the nearest food servers.

A crowd was waiting near a whole oxen being turned on a spit roast. Two turnspit dogs, one at either end of the spit, ran around in their wheels, turning the carcass above the fire that rested in a long brazier.

His family wasn't there.

He hurried through the crowd, moving from food stall to food stall.

There was no sign of his family as he worked his way down towards the Sini.

It had begun to snow, a light downfall, as he reached the intersection with the main river.

He glanced about, trying to workout whether it was better to head right or left.

Where are they? He screwed up his face. *I should never have left them. I—*

A gap appeared in the flow of people, allowing him an uninterrupted view across to the far bank of the Sini. A small boy in a miniature greatcoat like Isaac's, a little tricorn on his head, stood stuffing some form of bread-and-meat into his mouth.

Everett started forward, his progress almost immediately blocked by the flow of people. He pushed onwards, swerving around anyone who impeded his journey.

When a gap appeared again, the boy was gone.

Everett pushed forward, quicker now despite his exhaustion, casting glances around to find his son.

And there he was, walking away, hand in hand with a man and woman, neither of whom he recognised. Closer now, he could tell that the boy was too tall for Isaac.

A mess of thoughts blasted through Everett's mind.

Where...

I've lost my family.

Well done, sir.

All I've managed...

Where are...

And all because...

Well done.

... to do is annoy Renard.

I thought...what?

Where are they?

His mind screamed.

He stomped his foot down, the force nearly causing him to slip over on the compacted snow.

His mind screamed again.

The Down Hibourne ditch, Palace district

Kemp had remained in his regimental livery, needing the appearance of authority it would give him to investigate the nonsense that had gone on. The Hibourne above the bridge was quieter now. Although some families had remained, many had departed, no doubt to discuss what had happened and how to capitalise on it.

Kemp walked across the snow-covered ice to where a set of servants stood back from where their red-coated employers were skeeting, most of the Scarlets trying to consume food and steaming goblets of wine as they did.

Kemp came to a halt thirty or so foot off from the edge of the congregation and tried to catch the eye of a young maid. Another maid next to her realised he was watching and jabbed the first maid with an elbow. A whispered conversation ensued, punctuated by giggling. Finally, the first maid hurried across to Kemp.

"What can I do fa ya?" The maid asked.

Was she playing up her voice for him, dropping the polite voice she would no doubt use around her mistress?

"Just wanted a quick word. Nothing too worrisome," Kemp said, keeping his voice light, conversational.

"Go on," the maid said, raising her eyebrow knowingly.

Not today. "I was hoping you might know someone? Or know of someone rather."

The question caught the maid off-guard, her brow creasing between the eyes slightly with puzzlement.

"It's part of our investigations."

"To do with the attacks?" The maid's voice had become low, conspiratorial.

What's she after? Kemp nodded, trying not to look cautious.

"What do you know?" She was leaning in, her eyes wide, expectant.

"Can't really talk 'bout it."

The maid pouted.

She trying to harvest me for gossip?

When Kemp didn't respond, she took a step closer, touching his elbow.

Or trying to find out for your master or mistress?

"I won't tell," the maid said.

Ya need to get better at it if ya are. "I'm sure ya won't, but my captain'll hand me my arse."

"They'll never know."

"Really?"

The maid nodded, thinking that she was going to get her way.

"Truly?"

The maid nodded again.

"It's the stabbing."

"Why did they attack him?"

Kemp tapped the side of his nose with a gloved finger.

The maid feigned insult at his coyness.

"Man named Burston." He wasn't telling her anything she wouldn't already know.

"Why?"

He looked off, biting at his lips, trying to feign an inner conflict.

She stroked his elbow again, attempting to reassure him.

"I need to speak to Theresa Canner."

"She left," the maid let slip.

"Shit," Kemp exclaimed beneath his breath, hoping his display of frustration would draw her in further. "Where'd she go?"

Before the maid could question him, he added "If I can speak to her, then maybe…ya know." He shrugged and gave a smile.

The maid's eyes narrowed with suspicion. "How'd I know you'll come back?"

"Ya don't accept promises?"

"Would you from a soldier?"

"It's the sailors ya have to watch." *Come on.* He tried a soft grin to try to ease her.

"What would make ya come back?" She said returning the easy smile.

Ya're trying to play me. Seems I have to play along though. "Chance to skeete with ya?"

She stood analysing him.

Kemp found it too easy to keep a straight face and not reveal that his promises were worth nothing.

The maid nodded. "A group went to find a tavern. Headed towards the Sini."

"One of the stalls?"

The maid shook her head. "They wanted out of the cold. 'Spect it was something like The Woodsman's."

Kemp was familiar with the tavern. It was on the banks of the Sini opposite the barracks, just inside the boundary of Leigh's Wood

"See —" The maid started, but Kemp was already walking away.

Palais de Vasini, Palace district

Burston stumbled as he took the final step down from the Palace into the snow. A small part of him whispered that he should just return to his office, that sitting there and doing his work would be far more productive than any alternative.

He glanced back up the steps to where a handful of the Palace Regiment stood guard, despite the Palace being almost empty of anyone of import. *I suppose the comte is still there*, Burston thought as he shuffled on through the snow.

He had thought of returning home or to the Fayre after the man from the Palace Regiment had spoken to him. But an anger had remained boiling within him knowing his assailant had been captured but not where she was held. He had searched out some Palace servants to see whether they knew the location of his attacker, but they had known nothing. The pain in his side had grown steadily worse as he walked about the corridors, each set of stairs descended or climbed had jarred his wounds all the more. The pain, along with the lack of information from the servants, had tempered his fixation. He'd returned to his desk, only to be reminded of his confrontation with the man from the Regiment. It had reignited the anger, and he'd grabbed his coat to search for his assailant.

The problem now that he was outside, though, was where would they have taken his attacker?

Burston wracked his mind for something that the man from the Regiment had said that would indicate where the assailant was. But he'd said nothing of any value.

He glanced about the grounds before him. Snow had begun to fall again and the air seemed more chill than when he'd been out earlier.

She's not in the Palace. At least nowhere I have been.

Prisoners would be taken to the police offices.

His stomach sunk at the thought of dealing with Fox's lot. It was a bad thought that Fox was the most likely to become the new commandant.

But she was captured by the Regiment...

Would they hand her to the Inspectorate or the Watch?

There was a logic to the idea that they would hand his assailant over to the police, but there was a nagging sensation in his head telling him that the Regiment weren't constrained to observe the agreed order of things.

No. An attack near the comte...

An attack so close to the Palace...

...

But where?

He wouldn't be able to get into the barracks. Although he'd give it every attempt if need be. But...where would they hold her where he could go?

He started to walk, unsure quite of where he was going.

There were the Palace stables and the docks and boathouse.

The boathouse first or the stables?

He turned slightly from his path, cutting across clean, untouched snow, aiming for where the boathouse lay beyond a large copse of trees.

The Down Hibourne ditch, Palace district

The woman — Claire — was still stood there. Still watching people wandering past.

She looking for me? Hat thought again. The thought had been on a constant loop in her head, since she'd wandered back down the Hibourne towards the Sini and caught sight of the woman. It must have been nearly half an hour.

Hat had seen her at a distance, a glimpse amongst the crowds. Hat had been tempted to run to her, to demand to know things. Know something about why things had happened like they had.

But when she'd tried to get her feet to move forward, they'd refused. She'd just joined the edge of a crowd watching a game of ball that had started, the leather ball hurtling between team members as the two opposition teams charged them.

The ball went high over the crowd as Hat watched Claire. The crowd shuffled out of the way as the players burst through the ranks of watchers, desperately trying to find the ball.

A woman went flying as a player shoved her out of the way. Two other players threw themselves at the first player, one missing and landing in the compacted snow, the other smacking into the first player's back and flooring her.

Three more players had managed to make their ways past the crowd. One dragged the player who had floored the first from where he lay, pulling him back across the ice, but losing his footing and falling flat on his back. The other two chased the ball, shoving at each other, shouting insults.

Hat felt a compulsion to go for the ball herself, wanting to grab it and throw it in a fire to see what the players would do. Based on previous experiences of the game, they'd dive right in after it.

Claire was looking in Hat's direction.

Hat turned, trying to make sure that Claire didn't have a direct look at her face.

Hat waited, wanting to turn back but knowing Claire would see her if she did.

More players streamed past, tackling and barging each other as they went.

As the ball got booted towards the far bank, the surrounding crowds parted in a hurry to avoid the rolling ruck of players. Some stall owners were pushing their livelihoods across the ice, to avoid the path of play.

Hat risked a glance back towards Claire.

She wasn't there.

Hat started forward, looking for some glimpse of Claire. Her innards twisted at the thought that Claire had gone, that she'd lost her.

The ball game was heading back towards her, the crowds swirling around, attempting to extract themselves from the paths of the players.

Hat stepped forward, pushing on towards where Claire had been.

Something flew past her face.

Where's she gone?

Where the fuck —?

Something clipped her shoulder, turning her sideways.

What —?

Something — someone — drove into her side.

She still couldn't see Claire as her feet went from beneath her, and she crashed into the ice.

People swarmed around her.

Feet stomped down near her face, clipping and kicking at her legs and arms.

Pain flared in a hand as a foot came down on it.

Hat yanked, trying to pull her limb in, but her hand was pinned.

She shouted out, demanding that the person move, but her voice was lost amongst the noise of the crowd too absorbed in the ebb and flow of the ball game.

Feet continued to kick and jostle her.

A shout went up from nearby.

Amongst the tangle of legs, she saw a man, old and withered, lying prone, his lined face, creased in pain as he was subjected to the same barrage of kicks.

Hat struck out with a hand, smacking the back of the leg that was pinning her hand.

The old man's face was bloodied now.

She needed to curl herself into a ball before she ended up in the same state.

She lashed out again and again, but the person pinning her was oblivious, too engrossed in the ball game.

Hat felt in a pocket, searching for her blade.

Someone tugged at her arm.

She jerked her arm away, trying to prevent herself from being pinned by that hand as well.

Someone was saying something, shouting at the person on her hand.

Then the hand that had been trying to take her arm was shoving at the person on her hand and then the others around her.

Hat grabbed the blade from her pocket, holding it tight, ready to slash out should anyone attempt to hurt her again.

The hand appeared again, trying to grasp her arm.

Hat slashed out on instinct, part of her mind telling her not to, but her arm lancing out anyway.

The hand recoiled.

And then she saw the face.

Claire looked down at her, eyes wide with bewilderment.

Claire offered her hand again, and Hat took it with her uninjured hand. She held the other one close, trying to protect it against her chest, the intense throbbing taking over much of her mind.

She was on her feet now. She knew that.

And Claire…

Claire was pulling her away.

Hat stumbled on behind her.

The Sini River

I should just go home, Everett thought as he continued to scour the Fayre for his family. *At least I know they have to be there at some point.*

But he continued on.

His search had been disrupted by the ball games that had erupted amongst the crowd. He believed that there were at least three games in progress, but it was difficult to tell as they shoved their ways through the crowds, at times seeming to merge into a single game before separating again. He'd have hoped to have been away by now. The ball games always descended into a ruckus and it was something to which he had hoped not to subject his family. But it seemed that letting himself become distracted by other things had destroyed that hope.

His stomach had begun to grumble at him more and more as he searched, and was now aching. Everett had not wanted to stop his search to feed himself, and, anyway, it was punishment for his stupidity and his neglect of his family.

I should never have looked for that girl.

She'd be in prison now, in all likelihood. And then in a day or two she'd be a frozen corpse outside Sullivan's Court.

The thought that he might have saved her life did little to comfort him.

Someone shouted at him.

He looked, hoping it was one of his sons.

But it was just a man trying to sell him a warming bottle for his pockets.

Everett scowled, then felt guilty for being so harsh in his response.

He hurried on, turning into the Up Hibourne.

And there was a young girl stood handing money over to a chestnut seller, a bag of chestnuts in the other hand.

His daughter.

Amelia.

Everett stepped forward, ready to call to his daughter.

About him the crowd changed, more tightly packed now, pressing back towards the stalls.

Everett was shoved, his feet nearly going from beneath him. He scrambled, reaching out to support himself on whatever was near — a young boy.

Everett crashed to a knee, losing sight of Amelia.

Where is she?

He pushed himself forward, stumbling back up onto his feet, and nearly slipped over again.

Where is she? Images of Amelia being trampled under the feet of the crowd crashed through his mind.

Damn stupid man. Should never have left them.

They —

His thoughts were cut short by the sight of Amelia's golden braid amongst the crowd.

Everett rushed forward in the direction of the braid, pushing and shoving those that blocked his path, apologising profusely as he did.

A fist came flying at him.

He pulled back from its path, but it caught his chin.

Pain erupted in his face and then his side as he crashed to the ice again with a grunt and moan.

"Amelia!" He shouted out, hoping that he might be able to draw her to him. But his shout was drowned out by the noise of the ball game.

The tone though was changing. Shouts of support were turning to anger.

A man went down near him, victim to a punch.

It was turning violent.

I need to get to them, before...

Everett looked about, searching for his daughter's braid...

There it was, moving to the edge of the crowd.

Good girl.

Everett kept low, not wanting to gain his feet lest someone in the brawl saw him as a target.

Where's the Watch?

Would it be the Palace Watch or the Eldereham one here? Either way, they were lax.

Legs were striking him, sending jolts through his bruised body. But Everett still refused to get to his feet, shuffling on his hands and knees towards the edge of the crowd, in the hope that Amelia would still be there.

The blonde plait was ahead, seeming to cower away from the pressing crowd.

Everett thought he was about to break through when the crowd shifted again towards the girl who he hoped was Amelia.

The blonde plait dipped. The girl was falling beneath the press of the crowd.

Everett scrambled to his feet, not caring now if someone went for him. He shoved out with his hands, moving people from his path. His father's instinct pushed thought from his mind, replacing it with the simple drive to make his daughter safe again.

A figure was curled up on the ground, coat covered with powdered snow.

A man was pulling his leg back, ready to kick the prone form.

Everett dipped his shoulder, barrelling towards the man.

Everett bounced back as he struck the man.

But the man went toppling sideways, his half-raised leg not able to return to the ground quick enough to stabilise him.

Everett landed on his arse and slid back, striking into the legs of those that surrounded him.

Hands were grabbing him, but he pulled forward, scrambling for the prone form of his daughter.

He curled on top of her, feeling her small body quake beneath him.

She kicked out with her feet and shoved at him with gloved hands, but he held fast.

And then her grey eyes were looking at him and registering his presence.

Around him, the shoving and shouting and scuffles continued.

Limbs struck him, hitting existing bruises and sending shots of pain through his limbs.

"Where's your mother?" He whispered into Amelia's ear.

"I-I-don't know," Amelia said, her voice pitched high by her fear.

His stomach twisted.

One hand was close enough to let him stroke the back of her head in an attempt to calm her and himself.

Gunfire started.

The Watch.

Please be the Watch.

Except the Watch didn't carry guns. Only crossbows.

Everett held tight around Amelia, their erratic breathing becoming synchronised.

Where are you Anna?

VI

Palais de Vasini, Palace district

The boathouse had proven fruitless. Burston doubted anyone had been there since the snows had come. Travel was by horse and carriage only in winter. He'd thought that there was a better chance that they would hold his attacker away from where others might stumble on them.

I should have known, he chastised himself. Part of him wanted to blame it on still being shaken after the attack, but much of him didn't want to acknowledge that he was still shaken.

There was movement around the stables though. Two men were smoking just outside the door, smoke and breath entwining as they exhaled.

I'd have thought the stable hands would be down at the Fayre, not...

They were not stable hands. There was something about their posture, the way they watched their surroundings.

Regiment?

Burston slowed, unsure what to do. He was in the right place. If the Regiment were here out of uniform then they must have been guarding his attacker. Surely?

Could be off duty?

But then they'd be down at the Fayre?

I'm right, his mind insisted, trying to reclaim the certainty in himself.

The two men were watching him now, just looking at him approach, sucking on their little clay pipes.

Burston slowed until he was barely moving forward.

One of the men gave the slightest nod. A greeting?

"Aft'noon," the other man said. This one was taller than his companion, lanky and wearing a cap.

"Good afternoon," Burston said. Managing to get the words out emboldened him, and his pace increased.

"Thought everyone was down at the Fayre?" The taller man said.

"Not all of us abandon our posts at the first hint of a frozen river," Burston said. He felt himself straighten, unaware before that he'd been so stooped.

"True," the man said, straightening himself. The two men positioned themselves firmly in the doorway.

Do I tell them why I'm here?

What reason can I be here for other than to find my attacker? I could be after a carriage or a horse?

They won't let me through just for that.

The men looked at him, expectant.

"I believe you have someone to whom I wish to speak."

"I doubt it," the taller man said.

Burston's body tensed, his mouth flexing into a momentary snarl. "I will speak with her."

Burston stepped forward but found the shorter man putting his hand on Burston's chest. There was no pressure from the hand, but the intent was clear.

Burston lifted a hand, ready to swat the man's hand from him if it was required. "She attacked me."

"We wouldn't know about that," the taller man said.

Burston could make out sounds from inside the stables. The jingling of reins. They were preparing horses. They were moving her.

Burston's hand lashed out at the shorter man's wrist.

But the shorter man's other hand shot across and caught Burston's hand, twisting.

The shorter man pushed, catching Burston round the ankles and spilling him to the ground.

Burston gave a yelp of shocked pain, then bit down, trying not to show weakness, trying to scramble for his feet.

The shorter man still held Burston's wrist, twisting further and further.

"There's no one here for ya to talk to," the taller man said.

Burston flinched.

The taller man lent in to Burston's ear. "Ya gonna be sensible?" He whispered.

Burston tried to stare the pair of men down, but they maintained their resolve.

How dare they do this to me?
I am the victim here.
How dare they…
How dare they…

Burston nodded.

The shorter man eased his grasp, letting Burston regain his feet.

The taller man flicked his hand in shooing gesture, indicating for Burston to leave.

Burston stepped forward, but found the shorter man's hand on his arm again, holding tight, ready to twist.

Burston looked between the two of them. His face burned. He could feel his flesh trembling all over.

He turned, and, with flesh still trembling and face still glowing with rage, he hobbled from the stables.

Their superiors shall hear of this.
They will be made to pay.

The Woodsman
River Street, Leigh's Wood district

The tavern's air was hazy with smoke. Three separate fires burned in hearths set about the taproom. The wise had made their ways here early and claimed their places by the fires to keep the frozen outside as a distant memory. The later arrivals were forced to crowd as close as they could.

Although many of the patrons did not wear their politics, those that did were in red. There was not a single blue item of clothing in the place, Kemp noted as he stomped the snow from his boots after entering the establishment.

A barmaid was already weaving through the crowd to take his order. As he watched the crowd, trying to work out how best to locate Canner, he tossed the barmaid a coin and asked for whatever beer was the warmest.

There were pockets of Scarlets scattered throughout the tavern, placed, it seemed, wherever space had been left by those who had arrived earlier. As the ebb and flow of patrons changed, Scarlets would break off from one group and join another.

The barmaid arrived again with his pint.

"Ya know which one is Theresa Canner?" Kemp asked as he took the ceramic mug.

The barmaid shrugged.

Worth a try.

Kemp scanned the groups of Scarlets. Most were mixed, but a few were solely men and another was solely women.

He headed for the group of women in red, guessing that it offered the greatest chance of finding Canner on the first time of asking.

The group fell silent at his approach, their faces becoming serious.

"Sorry to disturb," Kemp said.

"I'm sure you are," one thin-faced woman replied. Her hair was tied tight into a ponytail by a long black ribbon. She held a goblet of steaming wine between the fingertips of both hands. Her grey eyes were cold and dull.

"I'm just looking for a Theresa Canner."

"You have a message for her?" The thin-faced woman asked.

"I'm not a messenger," Kemp said, trying now to scowl.

The thin-faced woman looked him up and down, raising an eyebrow. "Then why do you wish to disturb her?"

"I'm investigating," Kemp said. *Is this Canner? Is she just playing coy?*

"The Regiment do not investigate."

"Matters like this we do," Kemp said, hoping that his bluff wouldn't show.

"If I were to accept your claim, what would you be investigating?"

"That, I'm afraid, is for Miss Canner."

The thin-faced woman stared at him. "And if I were Canner?"

"Then I'd hope that you'd be more willing to talk," Kemp said.

"And why would you assume that?"

"'Cause it's in your interest to find out why someone tried to kill ya."

The thin-faced woman's eyes shot sideways.

"I am Theresa Canner," a shorter woman said. She looked older than the thin-faced woman, but her face was gentler, her look less severe. Her blue eyes shone amongst the low light of the tavern. "Is this about the unfortunate incident earlier?"

Kemp nodded.

"How is the poor man?"

The other women in the group had begun to depart, all except the thin-faced woman, who continued to watch the exchange.

"He survived," Kemp said, keeping his voice low now they were discussing the incident so indiscreet ears didn't overhear.

"Has the attacker been caught?"

"No," Kemp said, lying as he knew that if he revealed the attacker had been caught then Canner would just close up thinking that there was no need to provide any information. "Seems though the attacker wasn't after who they stabbed."

Canner glanced to the thin-faced woman, who remained passive. "And how you do you know this?"

"Why would a Scarlet go for some Palace lackey?"

"Why would a Scarlet attack another Scarlet, if that is what you are implying?" The thin-faced woman asked.

Kemp held back a scowl at the interruption. "Maybe Miss Canner can answer that question?"

"I have no idea. I did not recognise her," Canner said.

"You know it was a woman?"

Canner nodded. "I suspect it was someone who wore our colours, but did not share the beliefs," she said, looking to the thin-faced woman again.

"Who would have reason to send someone for you?"

"I have no idea. Other than the 'Fishers have a tendency for violence. A seigneur hung for it."

This all it is? 'Fishers going for Scarlets like they did last autumn? Something didn't seem right with this though. The violent rivalry between the 'Fishers and Scarlets was an established part of the city, but why would the attacker keep quiet for a 'Fisher when they were going to hang anyway?

"Was that your question?" Canner asked.

"So which 'Fisher?"

"They are all the same."

"They all hire someone to do their killing for them?"

Canner's face dropped, momentarily stunned that he'd challenged her suggestion. "Some…some may," she managed.

"And you believe this is what they did now?"

Canner looked to the thin-faced woman.

Why d'ya keep looking at her?

"And the man from the Palace just happened to be in the way?"

"Yes." Her voice lacked confidence. She still watched the thin-faced woman.

"But why didn't she go for you after seeing her mistake?"

"She had to make her escape."

It was a sensible suggestion, but it didn't sit well. The attacker wouldn't get paid for a failed attempt, so the incentive was to make sure that the true target did get hit.

No one in their right mind would hire someone to stab a worker at the Palace.

The intended target had to be Canner or another Scarlet, so why not stab them?

Unless making it look like a Scarlet was a target was the intent.

Canner still looked at the thin-faced woman.

Of course, Kemp's mind groaned. He turned to the thin-faced woman. "Next time ya might want to speak to me directly, Miss Canner." With that he turned and headed from the tavern.

The Up Hibourne ditch, Palace district

Everett and Amelia held each other tight as he tried to manoeuvre them around the outskirts of the crowd in their search for Anna and the rest of the family. Everett tried to ignore his aching and bruised body.

The gunfire had caused the crowd to fragment into groups, everyone trying to flee from the direction of the shots. This had led them, though, to cram themselves into tighter and tighter groups.

The gunfire had continued, almost as though the groups were being herded by the gunmen. Everett had only caught snatches of who the gunmen were, but by the glimpses of grey it seemed that it was the Regiment trying to assert some control on the ruck of the ballgame. At least it seemed that they were content firing into the air.

"Are you sure they were this way?" Everett asked Amelia.

Amelia looked at him wide eyed. She nodded. He hadn't been able to get a word from her since the gunfire had started.

Everett stroked her hair, as much to calm himself as her. "As soon as we find the others — and we will find them — it will all be fine. We will go home and have tea and crumpets by the fire, and I am sure we will be able to convince your mother to sing."

The words didn't bring the smile for which he'd hoped.

They hurried on through the trampled snow, swerving to avoid people running from the intermittent cracks of gunfire.

A grey figure stepped out in front of them.

Everett reared back.

It was one of the Regiment, musket shouldered. He held out his arms to his side. "Can't come this way," he barked at them.

Everett tried to swerve round him, trying to move Amelia so that he was between his daughter and the soldier.

The soldier shifted, blocking Everett's path again.

"I'm looking for my wife," Everett said, eying the musket.

"Ya won't find her here," the soldier said, keeping his arms out wide.

"She was this way. I need to get to her," Everett said, trying to bring himself to bear, to conjure forth the authority he used around the bank. It didn't come.

"Sorry, ya won't find her this way," the soldier said. "Everyone's leaving here before they trample each other to death."

"Your control of the crowd leaves a lot to be desired," Everett said, still holding firm.

The soldier's hand went towards his musket.

Amelia jerked in Everett's arms.

You won't shoot. You wouldn't dare.

"Ya need to move on," the soldier said.

Amelia quaked at Everett's side, as the musket's strap slid from the soldier's shoulder.

Don't do this. "My wife —"

"Will have to look —"

"My daughter is terrified."

"— After herself." The soldier's eyes did not shift from Everett's. The musket was now down at the soldier's side.

Amelia was trying to pull from his grasp, desperate to be away.

Everett took a step back. Then another.

The soldier nodded, but kept his eyes fixed on him.

Around them the masses continued their scramble to find refuge from their own stampede.

There was a crack of a musket some distance away.

Everett turned, and holding tight to Amelia, headed away.

I'm sorry, Anna.

River Street, Ferrymen's district

"I should take you to see a barber-surgeon or at least an apothecary," Claire said to Hat for the fourth or fifth time. No, definitely the fifth.

But the statement just caused Hat to flinch again, drawing her damaged hand into herself.

Hat had nearly clung to Claire as she'd aided the young girl from the melee of the ball game. The press of the crowd had forced them back towards the Sini, and it was only when they were some distance from the game that Hat had let go and then almost shoved Claire away.

They had found a quieter place up on the Ferryman's district bank of the Sini, and Claire had looked over Hat's injuries. Hat was bruised and her hand may have been broken, but it could have been far worse. At least they hadn't been near the other games from where gunshots could still be heard cracking through the air.

Hat stared at Claire, a hard look of defiance betrayed by winces of pain.

"You should at least find somewhere to rest, out of the way. Somewhere warm."

Hat didn't respond.

"I'll take you to a tavern. You don't have to talk to me."

Hat continued staring. The moment dragged on so long it surprised Claire when the girl finally spoke. "Why?"

"Because you're injured."

"Why ya helping me?"

"Because you're injured."

Hat stared at her in silence again, before she said: "Not a reason. No one helps just cause ya injured. Whatya want from me?"

"Would you be happier if I tried to get you to do something you didn't want to do?"

Hat just looked at her.

You trust people less than I do.

"I want you to have a drink with me."

"I don' do that stuff," Hat said, holding her arms tighter against her.

I'm not going to make you a prostitute. "That's what I want. A drink."

"But —"

"I rescued you."

Hat's head dropped. Her arms loosened. "Ya better be nice," Hat mumbled as she started to follow Claire.

River Street, Leigh's Wood district

Kemp stood on the bank of the Sini watching his fellow men of the Regiment herd the masses away from the Up Hibourne. Apparently it had reached the point of the Fayre when ball games had broken out.

At least it was one thing that made sense today.

The woman he'd caught was hired. He was certain of that.

Kemp sipped from his mug of warm ale. A gaggle of Scarlets had exited the tavern to watch the chaos on the Up Hibourne, and now stood around him, commenting on what was happening, tutting and complaining that it was the state of things with the 'Fishers in charge.

Who would hire someone to pose as a Scarlet to stab another Scarlet? And why not finish the job?

'Fisher's wouldn't stop from killing a Scarlet. Likely, the Ranters wouldn't either. So why run, and why do it in the open? When everyone was around?

Was it meant to disrupt the comte's announcement?

But why attack them not the comte?

Too much risk? Too well guarded?

As he continued to watch the crowds be disbursed, the Scarlets around him wittered on with their commentary, each word tensing his muscles.

What's happening?

Why did they do this?

The thoughts gnawed at him to the point where he just wanted to knock them from his head with one good slap.

I'm not part of the 'Spectorate. It shouldn't matter.

Just take the orders and do 'em.

But…

Why?

Why the…?

His face was warm, itchy. He scratched, realised he still had gloves on, removed them and then scratched again, letting his nails bite into his skin.

Need to find her.

She's the only one with the answers.

She won't tell me, the more practical part of his mind told him.

I need to know.

VII

Palais de Vasini, Palace district

Burston needed an officer of the Regiment. He had contemplated, for a moment at least, marching across the bridge to the barracks and demanding an audience. But the prospect of going beyond the Palace grounds had left him unsettled.

The Regiment's rooms in the Palace had been empty. The kitchens had only had a few privates and corporals warming themselves before going back out on patrol.

Was there no person of rank in the Palace? *Are my taxes paying for their enjoyment at the Fayre? For the officers to skeete while I'm trying to find answers?*

He had reached the main stairwell again and started up the steps. By all rights the Regiment should not have been beyond the ground floor, but given the lack of Palace staff no doubt some may have gone off nosing around the other floors, spying on what the baronies were up to.

Without his cane, Burston held tight to the bannister as he climbed, using it to lever his aching body up the steps.

There was chatter from above. Maybe a floor or two up.

Burston tried to hurry, to try to catch whomever it was, but his body protested, his legs refusing to move quicker.

He turned onto the landing and managed a shuffling run round and up onto the next staircase.

There was a flash of grey above. "Officer?" Burston shouted out. "Officer?" He started up the stairs.

The grey was out of sight.

"Officer!" Burston shouted again, turning the request to a demand.

His body was too sore, too stiff to keep up the pursuit.

Burston's footsteps slowed and each step brought a grunt of discomfort.

You better not have run.

He rounded the top of the stairs and started towards the next flight.

There was no man in grey.

Bastard.

Burston forced himself on. Maybe he could corner the soldier.

He came to the next flight of stairs.

And there was the man in grey, stood at the centre of the flight looking down at him.

"Yes?" The officer asked.

Burston's foot hovered over the first step. *I should make him come down to me.* "I need to speak to you," Burston said, looking up at the soldier, trying to make out the details on the coat to determine the soldier's rank.

"What can I do for you?" The soldier asked, not moving from where he stood.

A Divided River

You expect me to chase you? "You can —" He stopped himself, trying to force down his frustration at the Regiment not showing him due respect in the hope that a little reserve here might lead to a better resolution. The anger wouldn't go. "You can speak to me civilly and not make an injured man crane his neck like some pauper boy pleading for a scrap."

The soldier shrugged and took a few steps down, then stood expectant.

Burston gave a cough of displeasure.

"I do need to get to my orders," the soldier said.

"I wish to raise complaint," Burston said through gritted teeth.

"My —"

"I am an injured party."

"You need the Watch," the solider said — Burston could just make out a lieutenant's badge on his epaulets — taking a step up the stairs.

"I am talking to you. It is the Regiment who have my attacker in custody."

"Then they'll be handing them to the Watch and all will be well."

"I wish to speak to her, and your men have prevented me."

"My men?"

"Yes, lieutenant, your men. I demand to speak to my attacker." Burston's face was warming, anger tensing his jaw.

"My men are here in the Palace and aren't holding any prisoners." He turned and took another step up the stairs.

Burston stepped after him. "You cannot run away. Your men have a captive, and I will speak with her. And I want your men reprimanded for insubordination."

"My men do not hold prisoners." The lieutenant was walking up the stairs.

How dare you just walk away. Burston followed behind, his body protesting at the exertion. "Then why are they at the stables and refusing me entry."

"My men aren't at the stables."

"No…No.. They've probably moved her now."

"Who?"

"My attacker." *Wilful idiocy.*

The lieutenant had turned onto the landing.

Burston tried to walk faster, but already his breath was going from him, his heart racing.

"We don't arrest people. You need to speak to the Wat—"

"But you have her."

"We don't," the lieutenant called back. There was a clear distance between them now.

Burston rested against the post at the top of the stairs, hoping his heart would stop thundering in his chest soon.

He looked to where the lieutenant stood at the foot of the next staircase, staring back at him. Was the lieutenant smiling? Was there a smirk on his face?

Burston was sweating, his clothes sodden and clinging. He sucked in breaths trying to calm his body, but it would not unclench.

If he'd had his cane he would have thrown it at the lieutenant.

"Why do you want to speak to this person you think we have?"

"To —" Burston sucked in another breath. "To…To find out why."

"Does it matter?" The lieutenant asked as he start to stride up the stairs.

"Yes!" Burston screamed at him. "Yes!"

Why would someone have the nerve to attack me? Why would they put a blade into me? Why?

His anger drove him forward but, within a matter of steps, his legs buckled, the strength going from him. He collapsed to his knees, reaching out to steady himself against the bannister that ran the length of the landing.

Breath wouldn't come, his throat constricted to nothing.

White lights pricked his vision. Sweat stung his eyes.

He fell forward, one hand reaching out to stop himself collapsing fully, the carpet burning his palm as it skidded across in its attempt to break his fall.

He heaved as he stared at the floor, the flower pattern dancing.

Burston found a breath, the harsh intake causing his body to judder.

With each further breath, his body calmed.

The bastards.

The...Damn...Damn them to the graves of the deities.

The Woodsman
River Street, Leigh's Wood district

Hat held the tankard in her hand, eying the other patrons as though she expected someone to take it from her at any moment, her swollen injured hand held close to her body.

Do you really need to be that scared? Claire thought as she sipped at her own beer.

Despite the warmth of the tavern, Hat still looked cold, her body shivering every few moments.

"How're you feeling?" Claire asked.

Hat glared at her. "Thought ya said I didn't have to talk?"

"You don't. But I still get to ask questions."

Hat's lips curled into a momentary scowl, and she looked away towards the door. A fresh batch of patrons was arriving, seeking sanctuary from the cold and the continued frenzy down on the river.

"What do you do?" Claire asked.

Hat remained silent, still watching the door and sipping at her beer.

"I'm guessing that you're a seigneur's daughter who has run away."

The scowl reappeared.

"You're very serious."

"Whaddya think I do?" Hat said, turning to face Claire. Her eyes glistened in the gloom of the tavern despite the hardness in them.

"You stole from that man."

Hat nodded.

"Who for?"

"Me."

"Just you?"

"Keeps me alive."

"You didn't answer my question."

"No."

"No, you didn't answer my question, or no, not just you?"

Hat scowled again looking away.

I'm no threat to you.

"Ya get something out of this?"

"What?"

"What ya asking me all this? I tell ya, then what happens?"

"It depends what you tell me."

Hat rolled her eyes.

"I don't know what happens without knowing what's going on."

"Why'd ya care?"

"Because you need help."

"Ya know that for sure? Seemed to have survived so far without ya?"

"Is that what you're doing, surviving?"

"Lot of people out there who are just getting 'long, surviving. Why me?"

"You're the one I found."

"All ya need to do is put ya hand out in front of ya and ya'll find someone to help, if that's what ya wanna do."

Claire could feel her face reddening. *Why her? Be honest.* "You're the one who caught my attention."

"'S'pose I should feel happy 'bout that?"

"You can feel how you wish."

"You're annoying."

"Probably," Claire said, watching Hat sip at her drink, watching the other patrons, flinching whenever one came too close. *What's — who's — made you so frightened?* "What do you do?"

"Eh?"

"What do you do to survive?"

Hat shrugged, her face dropping to a sullen frown. She sipped at her drink again. She'd nearly be through her mug of beer.

"Is it just you?"

Hat cringed, causing her hand to jerk and slopping beer over the side of her mug.

Claire had thought it was the question, until she looked at where Hat was staring.

The tavern door had opened and a man had stepped in, taking a tricorn from his head. A young girl, no more than eight years old, stood hand in hand with the man, clutching tight to his arm.

It was the man who had aided Hat.

Everett looked about the tavern, getting the lay of the land, making sure that it would be safe for both him and Amelia. There was no sign of any large congregations of red or blue, which was at least something.

He had decided to bring Amelia to a tavern out of the way until the ruckus on the ice had calmed down and it would be safe to search for Anna and the others. He could only hope they were out of the way of danger. Hopefully, the warmth of the tavern and a good beer or two would help relax the icy knot that his stomach had become.

Amelia's grip tightened as a group of men brushed past them to go out through the door. One carried a leather ball.

Don't start another match.

He realised he was gritting his teeth, trying to keep himself from uttering something, and relaxed his jaw as much as he could.

Everett looked about again, trying to find a small corner they could hide in and drink in peace.

But there they were — the girl and the blonde woman.

Are they friends?
Who is she?
Who are they?

His mind began to reel with questions, adding this new sight to all that he'd seen that morning when he'd helped the girl and his sightings in years past.

I should go over and —
No.

He looked down at Amelia at his side.

She stared back, confused, her body still trembling against him.

I can't leave you, he thought at his daughter.

But they're there. They're cornered. I can find out. I —

Amelia's eyes glistened and then a tear slipped from her eye. Her lips trembled.

Everett, thoughts of the girl and the blonde woman fleeing, crouched and gathered his daughter in his arms, stroking her back in the hope of comforting her.

Slowly her trembling body stilled.

As he continued to hold her, he glanced across to see that the girl and the blonde woman were looking at him.

He glanced away, trying to use Amelia to block their view of his face.

Everett could feel his face warming. *Do not come across, please. Do not come across.*

He quickly rose from his crouched position, causing Amelia to stumble back in shock at the sudden change, and started towards the far corner of the tavern where he hoped he might find somewhere to hide before the girl and blonde woman could follow him.

Bridge Street, Banker's district

Where'd the fuck they go?
What road would they take?

Kemp pushed his horse on through the intersection and onwards through the Banker's district to Eldereham. It would have been easier if the river hadn't been frozen. They would have taken the prisoner by boat, and he'd have been able to just follow the path of the river.

When he'd arrived back at the stables, he'd found the stall empty and a carriage gone. He was certain, in that moment, that they were heading for Rivergate gaol. He'd saddled a horse and sped from the stables, hoping that his ride would keep its grip in the snow. He had no idea what he'd do when he found the carriage, but he knew that he had a better chance of speaking with the prisoner and finding out what she knew if he was able to get to her before she was lost in the gaol. The immediate problem, though, was working out which route they would have taken through the winding streets of the city.

They would not want to risk being seen, Kemp reasoned as he pushed the horse through another intersection and then followed the road to the right. It meant they would likely have avoided going over the Old Town Road bridges as they would have been too close to the festivities on the Hibourne. That would mean taking the bridge in Banker's, which would be silent with the Fayre in progress, and then travelling through Eldereham to the bank of the Sini and crossing into Sovereign's Gate before following the river up into the small portion of Rivergate on the east side of the Sini.

It appeared not all had gone to the Fayre, a group of people, done up tight in their winter coats and huddled into each other, were walking down the street. They glanced up as he sped on towards them, no doubt wondering what a soldier of the Regiment was doing chasing through the near-abandoned streets.

He was on The Crescent. The broad street through the centre of Eldereham curved ahead of him, the lines of boutiques and cafés closed, the homes amongst them shuttered against the cold.

As he continued round the long bend, a carriage came into sight. It was simple, non-descript, almost a box on wheels. The sort of thing that wouldn't draw attention amongst all of the other carriages that travelled the city on a daily basis.

He sped on, his horse reluctant at first, but a smack from his crop encouraged it to risk its balance on the snow-covered cobbles.

The driver, perched on top of the carriage, turned. It took a moment for the driver to realise that he was being pursued, but then he flicked his wrists, snapping the reins and driving the horses onwards.

The carriage headed away, but Kemp continued to gain.

Then the carriage was turning, heading into a side street, skidding in the snow as it changed direction.

Kemp readied to take the turning, slowing his horse for a moment, before geeing it on into the new street.

This street was narrow, leaving little room for the carriage to manoeuvre.

Kemp continued to gain. He'd need to get in front if he hoped to stop the carriage's progress, but the street was too tight.

The street didn't seem to end, the carriage just trundling on and on.

His horse was tiring, its breathing heavier, the cold weather no doubt exhausting it.

The carriage was beginning to edge away again. One building away. Then two. Then three.

A stumble appeared in the horse's gait. He needed to stop. If he forced the horse on, it would trip and throw him.

Fuck.

Kemp pulled the horse to a standstill, the carriage carrying on along the street and then turning into another side street.

The Woodsman
River Street, Leigh's Wood district

Hat had stayed for a second beer. It was promising. Claire had managed to get her to talk about the Fayre. It was only in broad terms — what she liked about it rather than what she was doing there — but she was talking. And she seemed to have forgotten the man-who-had-helped-her's presence in the tavern.

"Have you ever skeeted?" Claire asked. She'd switched to rum for her second drink. It would start to fog her mind if she had more than one, but she'd found some of the techniques Jacob and she had learned could be used to retain at least a veneer of sobriety.

Hat smiled, her eyes going wide. A genuine look of excitement. She nodded.

"Would you like to go today?"

The smile faded. Hat sipped her beer. "Ball games." The note of dejection was strong in her voice. She cupped her injured hand with her other, grimacing.

"True," Claire said. "What would you like to do?"

Hat shrugged, her sullen look now returned in full. "S'pose I'll need to go soon."

"Why?"

Hat looked at her. Her eyes were rimmed with moisture. "It's been nice, like, chatting with ya."

"But you have places to be?"

Hat nodded.

"Where? Can I walk you there?"

Hat's face hardened, but there was a note of fear in her eyes, a slight tremble to her body.

"I'd like to talk again."

Hat didn't respond.

"Maybe take you skeeting tomorrow."

Hat's lips pursed as though she wanted to say something.

Please.

"I'll meet ya here, tomorrow?" Hat said, head bowed, glancing up after she'd spoken, her eyes pleading with Claire.

"It's difficult to meet in crowded places."

"I'm sure we'll —"

"I wouldn't want to miss you. To miss going skeeting with you."

Hat's lips thinned as she thought.

Please.

"Ya know Runt Street, down in Southgate?"

"I can find it."

"There's a long alley that leads down to the river. I'll meet ya in there at the Runt Street end."

"I'll see you there at Eight."

"Six-thirty," Hat said, her voice insistent.

"Six-thirty. And we'll go skeeting."

"'Kay."

Claire offered her hand.

Hat looked at it, a little perplexed, then shook it.

The Up Hibourne ditch, Palace district

Everett's glance shot to the left. Every movement he caught in the corner of his eye was drawing his attention. *Where are they?*

Everett had not wanted to move until he was sure that the girl and the blonde woman wouldn't see them, but, with them positioned along the route out of the tavern, he'd have needed a large group to move through the centre of the taproom to help block the view of his and Amelia's movement. The large group had never come, and Everett had been left sitting with his daughter, both growing restless at not being able to start the search for Anna and the rest of the family. Each moment that passed meant that it grew closer to dusk and darkness, adding more urgency to their need to leave.

Amelia's legs had started swinging as she became restless, and she'd repeatedly kicked Everett in his legs to the point where he knew he'd have bruises come tomorrow morning. He had wanted to tell her to stop, to be a good child, sit peacefully and maybe they could talk about something that interested her, like her horse riding or music. But he couldn't tell her off. Not with her mother and brothers and sister missing. And he'd lost his willingness to talk, and, by the way that Amelia sat staring at her own hands, she had lost interest in conversation as well.

So they had waited, with Everett's calves becoming more and more bruised. And then the girl had left. The blonde woman had waited a few minutes to finish her drink and had then exited too.

Everett had taken Amelia's hand and, with no resistance from his daughter, led her from the tavern. They'd hurried through the crowds that now clung to the bank and sides of the river, finding their way back to where he had found Amelia. The stall had gone, but he hoped that Anna would have thought to come to this spot.

Unless she came here before us and waited and we didn't arrive. Maybe she is searching around. Or has gone back home.

Or was injured in the ruckus.

His stomach lurched at the thought.

"Where was your mother when you came to the stall?" Everett asked his daughter for the second time.

Amelia pointed off to their left.

"You are sure?"

Amelia nodded. "Where is she?" Amelia asked, her voice nearly breaking with fear. Tears were in her eyes again.

Everett crouched and drew her into his arms. He wished he could cry like her. But he needed to be brave for his daughter at least.

Slowly, Amelia's body stilled.

And then she was pulling from him.

He held her tight, trying to comfort her more, trying to stop her fear from overcoming her.

"Father. Father, please. It's…" Amelia sounded excited, not scared. "Mother. She's here."

Everett pulled away from his daughter, his mind trying to comprehend what she'd said.

She was staring off into the distance behind him.

He turned.

His eyes blinked against the snow that had begun to fall again.

Through the drifting whiteness walked Anna, leading the rest of his family towards her.

Everett gathered Amelia towards him, but she struggled against him, trying to head for his wife. But Everett held her tight, lifting her up into his arms and carrying her with him as he started towards his family.

We can head home. We find a cab in Eldereham and head home.

Thank... His mind refused to think the expletive.

VIII

The Down Hibourne ditch, Palace district

The first pinkish light of dusk had begun. Already the stalls were packing away, the crowds — their trade — being forced to the banks by the Regiment and the Watch because of the ball games.

Claire remained, huddled into herself against the fresh snowfall as she continued to wait.

He isn't coming.

Or he's already been.

I should come back tomorrow.

Jacob would come. He'd never missed a meeting before now. It was too important. She'd just been distracted. He'd turned up when she was dealing with Hat or the comte's announcement.

We'll have a lot to talk about tomorrow.

He'll turn up tomorrow. He won't just give in after not seeing me on one day. He'd want to make sure.

No point in waiting. Not now.

We'll skeete near here tomorrow. Then I can watch for Jacob.

She started off towards the bank.

He'll come.

He will.

But her mind conjured up images of his cough. The bloodied phlegm.

He will come, she tried to insist to herself.

He will.

She forced the images of the cough from her mind, despite the sinking sensation at the knowledge that if she hadn't seen him here, Jacob was likely dead.

Runt Street, Southgate district

Dusk had come and the world had quickly become dark. The lamplighters didn't bother with what few lamps there were in Southgate during winter. Hat slid along the frost-covered street, imitating skeeting as much as she could, practising for the next day. It was bitterly cold now that the sun had gone, but Hat was barely aware, thinking of the next day out on the ice. She'd need to find some way to get away from Claire later in the day so she could go about her business — not that business would be easy with her injured hand — but it would be fun to go skeeting for a little while.

Lamplight cast an eerie glow from the windows of the house as she made her way down the street, passing the alleyway where she'd meet Claire the next day.

A shadow moved around, temporarily blocking the light in a window.

It was enough to destroy Hat's thoughts of meeting Claire.

The Barker.

Hat came to a stop. She could just turn around, not bother going back tonight. She'd done it before...And received a beating for it. Not off the Barker, never off the Barker, but off Mabe. She'd used the skillet the last time. Nearly broke Hat's arm. And, anyway, she'd freeze to death in this cold.

She had to go in.

Hat's feet accepted the inevitable.

She could already hear the Barker's voice, the walls too thin to muffle it completely. He was shouting his usual string of obscenities and insults at whoever had received his wrath.

Could sneak in. Maybe he'll miss me.

Her hand rested on the door handle, ready to push.

She felt sick, vomit touching the back of her throat, causing her to cough.

Just need to get through tonight. Then tomorrow I can skeete.

Ya hear that Hat…Just tonight. Just one night, and then I can skeete and it won't chip into the Barker's earnings. Claire'll pay and all…

The door was wrenched from her hand as it was flung open.

The Barker, thickset and stinking of rum, loomed over her. Drool dribbled down his thickly stubbled chin. Then spittle was flying as he opened his mouth to let the expletives fly.

His hand was on her shoulder dragging her in, casting furtive glances up and down the street as he did.

The Sini River

The frozen river was different after dark. Gone were the masses trying to cram in and share in good cheer, replaced by groups huddled round braziers, warming hands and casting suspicious looks at any who passed by them.

It was not a place for a person of Burston's position. But what was his position now, he kept asking himself as he wandered in the darkness between the braziers, hurrying as much as he could when people turned to look at him.

I'm damaged.
That bastard damaged me.
No one trusts me.
No one respects me.
All because of some bastard with a knife.

He had thought to return home, but the thought of returning to his rooms in Ferrymen's district just angered him.

He was out of sorts he admitted to himself. Too restless, too caught up in what had happened.

The bastard.
The bastard taking it away from me.
If I'm not safe amongst people of quality then am I safe at home?

His stomach lurched. He'd already thrown up once while walking the Sini. The heaving had threatened to tear his wound open again, and his side had been left throbbing.

Is this what I'm reduced to —
The bastard.
The bastard. Reducing me to —
How dare they?
How dare they damage me like this?
Taking away my respect.
A knife.
They took it away with a damn knife.

Burston stumbled, one foot catching in the other. He caught his balance before he fell, but his foot slipped forward, threatening to topple him again. His arms pinwheeled. He crashed to one side, letting out a squeal of pain.

He could feel the eyes from the groups around the braziers on him again.

Stop looking.

I'm not your entertainment.
Go away.
Stop looking.

He fought the urge to curl into a ball and righted himself, trying not to look towards where the people undoubtedly stared. He hoisted himself back to his feet and trudged on. He would get no sleep tonight.

Timothy Everett's mansion
Founders' Way, Besson's Heights

Isaac was giving Susan the run around, refusing to be taken to bed. Amelia was sat with Clara on the settee, her sister whispering something in her ear. They hadn't left each other's side since they'd been reunited on the Hibourne. Everett's elder sons were settling their families into the guest rooms. It had been decided that it was best to have the family together after the events of the day. Servants had been dispatched to collect clothes from his sons' homes for the next day.

Everett looked at the glass being offered to him by Todd, his valet. Brandy. Good for the nerves and for warming him up after the long, cold day. And maybe it would ease the aching in his body. Everett accepted the glass and took a seat in the high-backed chair opposite Anna. She was scanning the newssheets.

Todd removed himself to the fireplace where he gave it several vigorous pokes to enliven the flames.

Who is she?

After everything that had happened, he still hadn't received an answer to the mystery of the pickpocketing girl.

And who was the blonde woman? An accomplice?

Todd was at his side again.

Everett ignored him. *Or just someone trying to help?*

Why did she run from me? After I helped.
And why was she with the blonde woman if she wasn't an accomplice?

"Sir?" Todd asked.

Everett didn't respond.

Todd waited.

The images of the girl played through his mind as he looked at his own daughters. *Would they be like her?*

"Amelia, will you play for us?" He asked.

Todd was already moving from his position behind Everett's chair and towards the piano to ready it for Amelia.

Amelia looked at him, her lips pursed and eyes glaring with annoyance.

"It will help us all relax after the day," Everett said. He just wanted to hear something normal, something that wasn't the world outside.

Would we all be like that? He thought.

Clara whispered something in her sister's ear, placing her hands reassuringly on Amelia's. Amelia's look softened and the two sisters rose and walked to the piano.

The two girls sat at the piano as Clara selected some sheet music from a small sheath that Todd offered to Amelia and placed it on the piano.

Are we already like that? Are we just picking each other's pockets?

Amelia took a moment to compose herself.

Everett tried to force the thoughts from his mind, to concentrate on his family and the pleasantness of his home.

Haltingly, Amelia started. She struck a wrong key, took a moment to compose herself and started again.

It was Danois's *The Winter's Night Lullaby*.

The gentle, tick-tock rhythm of the music tried to sooth Everett.

Where the money rests, and with whom, sets the tone and our approach to it defines our morality. Do I believe that? Did I — do I believe — what I told Renard?

Rivergate Gaol, Rivergate district

Kemp tethered his horse at the trough outside Rivergate gaol. The land inside the prison's outer walls was a field of white, except for the tracks leading from the gate to the prison's front door. The carriage he'd been pursuing, it seemed, had come and gone. After the failed chase, Kemp's mount had developed a limp and he'd been forced to rest it for a time. Since then, he'd been cautious of pushing his mount too hard in case it injured the horse, not wanting to risk having to explain it away to his superiors.

The trough had a small bail of hay hanging from one side, half of it now spilled on the floor, no doubt by the carriage's horses. The water in the trough was ice, but, as Kemp was about to try to break it with his gloved fist, he realised it had frozen through. *Sorry*, he thought at the horse.

He patted the horse's neck absently as he stared at the iron-bound double door at the front of the building, trying to work out how he was going to get an audience with the attacker.

The Regiment would know he was missing by now. The end-of-day reports would have been done, and the others who had patrolled from within the crowds would be eating a good stew and drinking several mugs of beer. Even if he managed to get the meeting with the attacker, he would face a long journey through the frozen city back to the barracks only to face his officers. He hoped the journey would be worth it, that the attacker would provide some information, whether intentional or not, that would make some sense of what had happened on the Hibourne.

At least his uniform had got him past the guards at the front gate.

Kemp hammered at the gaol's front door, reckoning it would need a solid thump to be heard through the thickness.

After a ten count or so of knocking, he relented and waited, counting beneath his breath. He'd give them a count of sixty before knocking again.

He reached forty-seven before he heard bolts rattling and sliding.

The door opened.

A man, balding and his face creased with age, stared at him. His thin lips scowled. "Late to be here?" The gaoler said.

"Regiment business," Kemp said, attempting to move through the doorway.

The gaoler didn't move. His arms crossed.

"Someone was brought here," Kemp said.

"By your lot," the gaoler said, clenching and unclenching his fists.

Kemp gave a slight nod.

"Told me not to let anyone near 'em. Ya're included in that."

"Their orders were wrong," Kemp said, trying to muster as much authority as he could.

"How're I'm supposed to know that?"

"'Cause I'm saying."

"Bring me a captain, I might believe 'em."

"I speak —"

"Ya speak fah no one. No one's sent here ta be talked to."

The gaoler stepped back and slammed the door.

Kemp rushed forward ready to push the door open, but there was already the rattle of bolts being drawn across.

Kemp hammered on the door.

There was no answer.

Kemp slumped forward onto the door, first to his head, then twisting on to his shoulder and then to his back.

Why me?

He'd be reprimanded when he got back. If he were lucky, he'd be cleaning the privies for the rest of the winter. And he risked it all because he couldn't just let it go. He'd needed to understand why the stabbing had happened. What had been going on with something that didn't rightly concern him.

I'm a fucking idiot.

But why me?

The thought pressed in on his mind as he returned to his horse.

A red who wasn't a red. Taken ta Rivergate by the Regiment.

…

Are we hiding something?

He untethered his horse.

For who though?

Why would we want to hide something?

He mounted his horse and turned it round.

Another thought pressed in on his mind. The chain of command. He answered to his officers and they to theirs, all the way up to…

He shook the thought loose as he rode toward the gaol's gate.

The thought began to slip back in as he passed beneath the entrance's archway. *All the way to the comte.*

Are we hiding something for the comte?

He forced the thought away as he eased his horse back into a trot, trying to concentrate on the punishment that awaited him.

IX

The Sini River

Josephine Addams hurried through the avenue of darkness between the lit braziers on the Sini. She'd lost sight of Ellis and Berdine, who'd wandered ahead as they left The Woodsman. The tavern had been full of Scarlet's but the three young 'Fishers hadn't let that scare them off. Ellis and Berdine were carrying small pistols after all. That was until small groups of Scarlets had started to pen them in. It had been subtle to begin with — groups just shifting around with the normal ebb and flow of the tavern. But, one after another, the groups had closed in on the three 'Fishers, crowding round their small table. If only Ellis hadn't been so cold and demanded to warm up at the nearest tavern.

It had been Ellis, though, who had finally given in and led the way out, barging through the sea of reds. They'd laughed as the three of them had fled. It had made Josephine's face warm. She'd felt stupid. It had been stupid to risk going in there no matter how cold Ellis had been. She had debuted in the spring. She was supposed to be more aware of politics now, more aware of how she should manoeuvre within society. She wasn't bound to the house, and she had to remember that meant she had to act responsibly and not get into stupid situations. Or lose her money like she had that morning.

Josephine pulled her coat tighter around her, dipping her head against the wind that blew down the river, directly at her face. They'd find a cab in Eldereham and head home together. Berdine had offered for them to stay at her house for the night so that neither Ellis nor Josephine would have to risk travelling home by themselves.

Josephine glanced up, searching through the darkness for the silhouettes of her friends. She was sure it was them ahead, arm in arm, looking quite the couple despite neither having an interest in the other.

She glanced off to either side, watching the groups around —

Pain lanced through her side.

Something had been thrust into her.

And then there was another thrust into her other side.

As Josephine went to scream, a hand clamped on her mouth.

She threw an elbow backwards, trying to connect with her attacker. But the attacker was too close, and the attacker's arms were around her, holding her tight.

And the stabbing continued, in her front now.

Something thrust into her stomach, glancing off her corset's boning.

It came again, this time finding her flesh.

And the darkness was getting thicker.

She struggled.

It felt like she struggled at least.

She couldn't tell through the pain. Her body was just pain.

More stabs pierced her.

The darkness thickened and thickened. Until there was nothing to see, only the pain she felt.

And then nothing.

The figure that had broken away from one of the groups round the braziers and followed the young woman lowered the victim to the ground and pulled the knife from her stomach, wiping it quickly on the woman's coat.

Within moments the figure was running.

The victim's friends were too far ahead to notice. Those around the fires could see nothing that didn't fall within the light coming from the braziers.

The victim's friends would reach the Eldereham bank and realise their friend was not behind them.

They would backtrack but would not find the body in the darkness.

They would report her disappearance to a pair of Eldereham watchman patrolling near the bank, but they, too, would not be able to find the body. The people around the braziers would not see the body as they departed in the small hours towards the banks rather than the centre of the frozen river.

The body would only be found at dawn the next morning as the stalls began to reappear on the river preparing for the second day of the Fayre.

From *The Herald*

YOUNG KINGFISHER ASSASSINATED.

Vasini was struck with the horrifying news that Mademoiselle Josephine Addams, a Kingfisher who had debuted earlier in the year, was murdered in cold blood at the end of the first day of the Winter Fayre.

Her body was found on the frozen waters of the Sini River early yesterday morning, apparently remaining unnoticed by the Watch or people who frequented the river on the first night of the Fayre.

The investigation of this innocent's murder is already in chaos, though, as the body was found on the river between the Palace, Eldereham, Leigh's Wood and Ferrymen's districts. It is understood that without a commandant to provide guidance on which Inspectorate should lead the investigation, there is a dispute in regards to under whose jurisdiction the murder has fallen. A dispute that it seems Seigneur Gallieni of the Baronnie de Justice has yet to step in and resolve.

It is understood that Mademoiselle Addams had inadvertently attended a tavern that was being frequented by Scarlets. It is unclear at this time whether the murder is a continuation of the violence that erupted in the wake of the death of Dame Vittoria Emerson earlier in the year, or, indeed, was in some way linked to the revelations earlier in the day that several 'Fishers' loyalties had changed to support Philippe Reno.

The adventures of D![r underline]() Marcus Fox &
Elizabeth Reid continue in

The Vasini Chronicles II:
The Theatre of Shadows

The Winter Fayre Killer has escaped.

An ambassador lies murdered.

An ally is accused.

The stage is set.

Let the play begin.

Coming in 2018

ABOUT THE AUTHOR

Christian Ellingsen grew up first near treacle mines in Hampshire and then in the depths of the South Wales valleys. He attended the University of Wales, Lampeter, and Cardiff University, graduating with a BA in History & English and a MA in Creative Writing. After several jobs in community regeneration in one of the most deprived areas in Wales, he worked for the BBC, first on the Switchover Help Scheme and then in Radio Drama. He lives with his wife a stone's throw north of London. When he isn't exploring the flooded streets of Vasini, he's a bid writer.

You can find out more about Christian, *The Vasini Chronicles* series, the *Tales From Vasini* series, and his other stories at www.christianellingsen.net, and follow him at:
>www.Facebook.com/MrChristianEllingsen
>www.Twitter.com/mr_ellingsen

Available now

The Silver Mask
by Christian Ellingsen

Book One of
The Vasini Chronicles

The gods and goddesses are dead, killed two hundred years ago. With their destruction the moon split apart, the sun dwindled and the land was devastated. Civilisation has re-emerged from the carnage, but twisted creatures still prowl the savage Wildlands between the city-states.

In the skies above the city of Vasini, a falling star, a fragment of the dead moon goddess Serindra, heads to earth. In the Palace district, Dame Vittoria Emerson, darling of the city, has been found dead, lying amongst her own vomit.

As Captain Marcus Fox of the Inspectorate hunts the killer, Dr. Elizabeth Reid searches for the remnants of Serindra determined to make sure the poisonous quicksilver it contains is not used. With Vittoria's death threatening to draw the city's political elite into a war of assassins, Fox and Reid must rush to expose the secrets that lie within Vasini before they tear the city-state apart.

The Silver Mask is the opening part of The Vasini Chronicles, a series of flintlock-and-alchemy fantasy novels set in the city-state of Vasini.

The Silver Mask is available in paperback and as an eBook.

Available now

The City Between the Books & The Bridge People
by Christian Ellingsen

In The City Between the Books, Lex's time at university isn't going well and, on a cold November morning, things get worse. Searching the stacks of the university library, Lex finds that the books can lead to strange places, places that are maybe better left unexplored, especially if she wants to finish her essay on time.

In The Bridge People, Hannah's summer holiday has been spent exploring the woods and learning games from her grandparents. However, when her mother falls ill, Hannah goes on a quest for chicken soup in the hope that it will cure her. But, to get the soup, she'll have to cross the bridge to the shop. And there are things beneath the bridge. Horrible things, worse than any of her fairy tales, who scare even her mother.

This book consists of two stories: The City Between the Books (a novelette); and The Bridge People (a short story).

The City Between the Books & The Bridge People is available now as an eBook. Read on for an excerpt from the book.

I

The gust struck her full force, biting into her flesh.

Fuck me.

Lex thanked her fluffy socks. At least her feet were warm as the November wind cut through her coat and clothes. She sniffed and wiped away a trickle of snot. *Don't be a cold*, she told herself, she couldn't afford the flu that seemed to have gripped the campus.

She could see the library ahead. It would offer some warmth at least.

Least it's not raining.

She huddled further into herself, keeping her head down, and forced herself on through the wind.

Her stomach rumbled, protesting the lack of breakfast. She'd rushed out that morning, dropping some washing into the campus laundry room before heading to the library to try and get the books she'd need for the essay. She was almost certainly going to be late. She'd not realised the deadline was so soon. She'd had it in her mind she had another two weeks, but at the lecture yesterday they'd been reminded that the essays were due Friday. It had been too late to get to the library after the lecture, so she'd spent the evening fixing the hem of a skirt that had fallen apart on her. It would now be two days of rushed reading and half-thought-out writing. It hadn't been like this at school. During her A-Levels, everything had been on time. No racing at the last moment, no skipping lectures for one module so she could catch up on work for another.

Other students, in pairs and small groups, hurried around in discussion with each other, hunched over, their faces grey in the cold, eyes watering, noses sniffling with flu.

As she came to the library entrance, the doors opened and a group emptied out, oblivious to her presence, bumping her arms and elbows as they pushed past.

Lex ignored them. The door was closing on her as she stepped forward, hoping for the library's warmth.

But it was still cold.

She looked to the front desk where the librarians stood serving queues of students, all of them wrapped up in coats.

The heating couldn't be on, or it was broken.

Fuck.

She pushed at her nose again, trying to stem the growing stream of snot.

Lex stopped as she searched for a tissue in her pocket.

Someone grumbled at her from behind. She felt them swerve past and carry on, still grumbling beneath their breath.

She found the tissue and blew her nose.

She could go back to the halls of residence. There was heating there. But then she'd delay starting the essay.

It won't take long. It won't take long. I can cope if it doesn't take long.

Her body didn't want to move though.

I've frozen to the spot.

There was more disgruntlement from behind her, and her legs moved on.

Fuckers.

She pulled the slip of paper from a pocket, then removed her gloves so she could unfold it to read the list of suggested books for her essay on eco-feminist interpretations of US history. Ten books. If she could get four then hopefully they would be enough to at least produce an essay. Whether it would be any good would be another thing.

She headed for the bank of computers along the far wall, weaving amongst the flow of other students who seemed to move around the library with purpose, heading directly to shelves and grabbing the books they wanted within seconds.

Lex waited for a computer to become free. Twenty minutes passed. Once seated, it took another fifteen minutes to navigate the archaic search function to even begin looking up the books. The students at the other computers seemed to use it with ease, typing in their queries and getting the results and moving on within a few minutes. It took her another half an hour of searching to be certain that only three of the ten books were not on loan.

With their catalogue numbers written down on her wrist so she didn't have to take off her gloves, she began to search the stacks.

Looking under 'History' proved to be fruitless, as did 'Environment'.

By the time she'd convinced herself that the books weren't in either section, she realised another forty-five minutes had passed and that her washing was likely done.

She had thought it was cold in the library, but returning to the bluster of the outside reminded her how much colder it was out there. She puzzled over where she might find the books as she forced herself against the wind, the branches of the trees that lined the pathways whipping and waving about. She made her way to the laundry room only to discover that someone had already pulled her clothes from the washing machine — unceremoniously dumping them on a table — and started their own wash.

All of the tumble driers were loaded, but two seemed to have completed their cycles. Wanting to punch the machines, she removed the clothes, screwing up her face at touching other peoples underwear, and dumped them on the table, replacing the loads with her own clothes.

She fed the machines with twenty-pence pieces, steeled herself against the cold and hurried back to the library, the wind blowing her on.

She ran her tongue over her chapped lips as she stood in the library, watching everyone else find what they needed.

Lex had settled on trying 'Feminism' next.

She still hadn't found the section after twenty minutes, but had stumbled across 'Geography' — nowhere near the 'Environment' section on the mezzanine level — which had one of the books secreted in its own little sub-section. The other two were nowhere to be found.

Continuing her search for 'Feminism', she found 'Gender Studies' on the first floor, tucked away near the rear of the library, but there was no 'Feminism' section. The 'Gender Studies' section yielded no results, strangely having a sub-section dedicated to plays with male names in their titles.

As she scoured the lower shelves of the section again, hoping that she missed something, she slumped to the floor, sitting cross-legged, and stared at the one book she'd found.

Can I do the essay with one book?

She looked through the stacks at the clock on the wall, then checked it against the clock on her phone. Another hour had passed. Her clothes would be dry.

Lex's body shivered at the thought of going out into the cold — *Worse cold*, she corrected herself — but forced herself to her feet.

She had to wait ten minutes at the desk to check out the book, unwilling to leave it in the library in case someone else took it or, worse, she couldn't find it again.

Lex finally headed out into the cold, the wind biting through her coat once more.

She found her clothes in the tumble driers. As she pulled them and her dressing gown out, she held them against her face, using the residual heat to warm herself. Her bags packed, she lifted them on to her shoulders and headed back to the library.

Bulkier now with the bags, she was jostled more by the passers-by who coughed and sneezed at her.

As she pushed through the doors to the library, she just wanted to find one more book. Just one more, and she could go back to her room away from the flu-ridden people and the cold, and she would attempt the essay on what she had. She could do it with two books, she convinced herself.

But as she started to search the stacks, trying not to bash them with her bags, despair set in. The library just didn't make sense to her. Whatever classification system they used wasn't the Dewey Decimal, and seemed in places to be made up of two or even three systems. Books could be marked with strings of letters, or numbers or both. Hamlet was the unwieldy:

Ha.Sh
WX.51
5083.

0.097
2.XXX

A book on architecture — located next to a box of pamphlets on fertility deities — was the slightly less cumbersome:

40.74
84.73.
9857

Someone had even scratched out several of the codes with black biro.

As she traipsed along the same stacks for the third — no, fourth time, she realised — she wished she could just restructure the whole place. It was the only way it would ever begin to make sense to her.

And so she did. She grabbed the plays with the male names from the 'Gender Studies' section first, smuggling them amongst the clothes in her bag to make sure she didn't raise suspicions.

She lost track of time as she trafficked books around the library. As she did, she came across one and then another and then more of the books from the reading list. Apparently the computer was lying when it said all but three of the books were out on loan. Too caught up in her new endeavour, she didn't bother to check them out; she had them in her possession after all, she could finish her re-organisation and then take all the books she needed to do her essay.

Lex had congregated nine books on eco-feminist viewpoints of US history in the bottom left-hand corner of the stacks containing US history, themselves located in a small alcove in the almost abandoned lower level of the library.

As she stood back to admire her work, she realised she'd forgotten one book — the first one she'd found — and slipped it onto the shelf.

She stood back again and admired her work. Overcome by a desire to record the accomplishment, she pulled her phone from her pocket and held it up ready to take a photo.

As Lex looked at the screen, she saw a glow emanating from the paper-thin gaps between the books.

She glanced over the screen, concerned there was something wrong with her phone.

The glow was there.

It was real.

Lex tried to process what she was seeing, trying to come up with an explanation.

Her mind was blank.

She stepped forward, trying to peer behind the books to see the source of the glow.

The books were too tall or the shelf above was too low. Either way, she couldn't see the back of the shelf properly.

She reached out for the last book she had placed on the shelf, intending to remove it to get a clear look at the back.

Her touch pushed the book backwards. It slid then tumbled, falling behind the bookcase.

The new gap allowed through more of the thin, cold light.

How can it fall back? The wall would stop it.

She reached out. Her hand hesitated then touched the next book, pushing it back with a tentative finger. The book tumbled away.

There was a faint thud as it landed in whatever space the glow emanated from.

She pushed another book.

Then another.

Then she was shoving with her whole hand.

The books tumbled away, followed by tiny thuds.

She crouched to peer through the gap that now ran half the length of the shelf, trying to find the source of the glow.

Instead of a magnolia-coloured wall, she found herself peering at a lit, stone corridor. It appeared to descend after two meters or so, the lip of what may have been a staircase blocking sight of the light source.

What the fu —?

Lex found her hands were shoving more books from the shelves, controlled by the part of her mind that wanted to make sense of what she was seeing.

The shelves cleared, she found herself staring into the corridor. The only barriers now between her and the glow that emanated from down the stone steps were the bookcase and the layer of books she'd created across the floor.

How? Shit. How is this here?

I'm dreaming, her mind told her. She must have fallen asleep. She couldn't place when she'd fallen asleep, but she must have fallen asleep somewhere in the library, probably freezing her unconscious arse off.

Fuck. My essay.

I should wake up.

But the thought didn't bring back consciousness. The idea of dreaming was too much of an attraction.

Unsure she should indulge the dream, Lex looked at the bookcase, trying to work out how to get past. It was too heavy to move as a single unit, but it looked like the shelves were just resting on brackets.

She gripped one. There was no resistance as she lifted the shelf free of the unit.

She rested it against the next bookcase along and removed another shelf and another, until she had made a gap tall enough for her to pass through.

I should at least find out what's causing the glow. Seems wrong to waste a dream.

She went to step through and then remembered her bags of laundry. She grabbed them and, carefully picking her way through the pile of books, walked through the bookcase.

Now at the top of the steps, she could see that the staircase was a tight spiral, the centre empty, allowing her to gaze down into the receding glow.

Lex descended, her feet sending echoing steps ahead.

The glow grew more intense, and, as she continued down, she came across wall sconces with strange flames burning in the glass bowls they held. She stopped for a moment to watch the bluish-white flames flicker and dance as they sat on the clear liquid in the bowls. The flames let off a deep acrid smell. No heat came from them.

Lex descended further. The cold became more intense, a biting breeze becoming a gust becoming a stiff and constant wind howling up the steps.

It became too much, and she came to a halt, shivering and bunching into herself, turning her back on the wind to try to protect her face.

She wetted her cracking lips.

I could just go back to the library.

Lex looked up through the centre of the spiral at the steps that stretched up above her. It seemed a waste to go back. And she'd have to write her essay if she went.

My clothes.

Lex dropped the laundry bags to the steps and started groping through, searching for something she could use to warm herself.

She found a jumper that she slipped on over her coat, not wanting to take her coat off even for a second. Then, towards the bottom, she found her dressing gown. She tugged and pulled it, dislodging the clothes that sat on top, spilling pants, tops, socks and woolly tights to the stone steps. She wrapped herself in the dressing gown and then grabbed some red socks to put on over her gloves.

Gathering the clothes back up, she hoisted the bags back on to her shoulders and stuffed her hands into her dressing gown pockets.

Sharpness stabbed at her hand. She jerked it from the pocket.

A needle, a small length of black cotton dangling from the end, protruded from the ball of her hand. It was the needle she'd used to re-hem her skirt.

Scowling at it, she yanked it out and returned it to her pocket, then rubbed her hand to try and massage away the remaining pain.

Lex carried on, shoulders hunched, head bowed against the cold.

A few more turns down the stairs, and she found herself at a doorway.

The door, bleached white and cracked with age, was blown open, the wind howling through.

She hurried out.

Proof

71293419R00103

Made in the USA
Columbia, SC
24 May 2017